1-19-22

Scottish
Bakehouse
Mysteries™

In Grave Danger

WINTER FAIRE

Elizabeth Penney

Annie's®
AnniesFiction.com

Books in the Scottish Bakehouse Mysteries series

Library of Congress-in-Publication Data
In Grave Danger / by Elizabeth Penney
p. cm.
I. Title
              2021943346

AnniesFiction.com
(800) 282-6643
Scottish Bakehouse Mysteries™
Series Creator: Shari Lohner
Series Editor: Elizabeth Morrissey
Cover Illustrator: Kelley McMorris

10 11 12 13 14 | Printed in China | 9 8 7 6 5 4 3 2 1

1

The February wind might bluster and the temperatures plummet, but inside Superior Bay College's kitchen classroom that Sunday evening, all was warm and cozy. Better yet, the room was filled with the enticing aroma of roasting cacao beans.

Molly Ferris took a deep, appreciative sniff, smiling at her business partners and best friends, Carol MacCallan and Laura Donovan. The trio—known affectionately around Loch Mallaig, Michigan, as the Bakehouse Three—owned Bread on Arrival, a popular destination in the quaint, Scottish-themed town. When they'd learned that professional-level chocolate-making classes were on the Loch Mallaig Winter Faire schedule, they had jumped at the chance to learn new skills and have some fun. And eat lots of chocolate over the course of the four-day workshop.

At the front of the room, celebrity chocolatier and former local resident Devon Macintosh stood in a casual stance, muscular arms crossed. The camera operator, a young man with close-cropped auburn hair and a pleasant, freckled face named Cole Keith, hovered to one side, focused on catching the cable star's every move.

Devon's piercing blue eyes twinkled. "Listen carefully, class. I'm about to share the foundational concept that drives my business." All two dozen students seated at long tables leaned forward, and Molly exchanged excited glances with Carol and Laura.

After a dramatic pause, Devon went on, "If love had a flavor, it would be chocolate." He broke into a huge, handsome grin when the group of mostly women giggled. "You might say they're the perfect pairing."

"Especially on Valentine's Day," a woman seated up front said. "That's why I'm here. To make chocolates for my husband."

The camera operator filming the class for Devon's cable show swiveled his viewfinder toward the woman, who blushed and patted her hair. Interest in the class had skyrocketed when people learned it would be televised.

"Who else in this class is planning to make Valentine's chocolates for a loved one?" Devon's gaze swept the room. "Anyone want to share?"

Molly gave Carol a gentle elbow, hinting that she should speak up. They'd been friends since college, and the idea for the bakehouse adventure was sparked during their thirty-year reunion. Of the three friends, Carol was the only one who was married. Molly was a widow but in a relationship with a wonderful man named Fergus MacGregor, who owned the luxurious Castleglen golf resort. Always-single Laura was dating handsome widower Trent McKade, and Molly thought this one might stick.

Carol lifted a hand. "I'm going to try." Her resonant laugh rang out. "They'll probably come out as blobs, but hopefully they'll taste okay. Good thing Harvey isn't fussy." Harvey, a mostly retired journalist, enjoyed life in Loch Mallaig, especially the fishing.

"You'll be surprised how quickly your skills improve," Devon said.

Molly decided to chime in. "I'm also making chocolates for a special guy." Even the thought of him gave her a thrill that reminded her of the crush she'd had on him when they'd met as teenagers while she was vacationing in town. They had been friends for a long time, and in recent months had become much more.

"Nice," Devon said. "Is this special guy your husband?"

Molly felt her cheeks heat up at the question. She didn't quite dare to admit her deepest hopes. "No, he isn't," she finally said. "But we're very close." Now Carol gave Molly an elbow, communicating that she knew Molly's words were an understatement.

"I think all your loved ones are going to enjoy your confections." Devon made a discreet gesture toward his assistant, a plump, young woman with curly brown hair. After she fiddled with a controller, the screen behind the instructor lit up and music began to play.

The words *Devon Macintosh, Chocolates by the Bay* floated into place on the screen. Chocolates by the Bay was the name of Devon's famous San Francisco confectionery, as well as his show.

"Tonight, we're in lovely Loch Mallaig, a crown jewel of Michigan's Upper Peninsula," Devon said, speaking into the camera. "The UP is renowned for its natural beauty, outdoor sports, and wonderful hospitality." The audience burst into applause at his compliments. After the clapping died down, he went on. "Thank you for joining me for a special episode of Chocolate 101. With us are local residents eager to learn more about making chocolate—and to spend time with me." The group roared approval.

The classroom door squeaked open and everyone craned their necks to see who the latecomer was. Bakehouse employee and college senior Bridget Ross shrugged her shoulders in apology. She slipped into the room and, after glancing around, headed for Molly's table.

"Sorry I'm late," Bridget whispered, stowing her bag under the table. She picked up the apron at the place setting, which held the equipment and kitchen tools they would be using soon, and slipped it over her head. She smoothed her glossy black hair into place, which today sported a pink streak. She made a wry face. "My study group went long."

"You didn't miss much," Molly whispered back. "We're just getting started. I'll catch you up after Devon finishes his intro."

Someone in the room gasped, grabbing Molly's attention. Devon stood at the workstation up front, a machete in one hand and a large cacao pod in the other. With one swift, perfect strike, he split the pod down the middle. Holding up the halves to show the white, oval beans, he asked, "Who would guess what depth of flavor these beans hold? If they're processed correctly, that is."

As the class watched with rapt attention, Devon took them through the scientific process of making the world's favorite confection. While being carefully monitored, beans were fermented, dried, roasted, shelled, and ground to make a chocolate liquid. He illustrated each stage with a small sample.

"This is the magic stuff right here," he said, passing around a bowl holding a shiny, brown liquid. "Now a decision is made. Does it become cocoa powder or eating chocolate?"

"Eating chocolate," the class chorused.

Devon joined in the laughter. "All in good time. We're going to break for a few. Help yourselves to refreshments in the hallway and we'll reconvene soon to cover a key technique." He waited a beat, then spoke in a deep, mock-serious voice. "Tempering."

Everyone groaned and laughed again, chatter breaking out as the students stood and stretched.

"That was the most fascinating lecture on chocolate I've ever heard," Laura said. "I love to learn about the science behind food." Laura was a trained chef and head baker at Bread on Arrival.

"Me too," Bridget said. "And we're fortunate to have a great food scientist on the faculty here." She nodded toward a woman who seemed to be in her thirties, sporting a pair of red cat-eye glasses and glossy, light-brown hair pulled into a ponytail. Like everyone else in the room, she was dressed for winter in slacks and a sweater. "That's Dr. Dunbar, one of our professors, chatting with Devon and his assistant."

"Didn't Dr. Dunbar arrange to have Devon come for the faire?" Carol asked. "I thought I read that in the newspaper."

"Yes, she did," Bridget said. "Devon actually went to school here before moving on to culinary school. I heard that he's been friends with Dr. Dunbar since college."

"He's certainly done well for himself," Molly said as the small group moved in unspoken unison toward the classroom door.

"That's for sure," Laura said. "His show is one of the most popular on the cooking channel."

Molly eyed Devon, still talking to Dr. Dunbar. "I wonder if we can get a mention of Bread on Arrival in this episode somehow," she mused, her marketing wheels turning. While Laura and Carol did the bulk of the baking, Molly handled promotions and other day-to-day operations for the bakehouse.

"How about bringing treats for class refreshments tomorrow?" Carol suggested. "Maybe he would give us a shout-out."

"I like that idea," Laura said as they got into line for that evening's snack. "Doesn't the show usually feature local color from their location?"

"Probably why holding it now was such a good idea," Bridget put in. "The Winter Faire will provide lots of good footage. My friends who major in video production call it B-roll."

Laura's expression was thoughtful. "I'll come up with something really spectacular." She picked up a dry cookie, which was obviously store-bought. "I think we can do better than this."

Carol laughed. "No kidding. Who wants coffee? I'll pour."

"I'll take decaf," Molly said, echoed by the others.

The outside door at the end of the corridor opened, allowing a blast of cold air to enter as a short, burly man strode inside. He snatched off his wool cap, revealing a balding head.

"What's Blane Tully doing here?" Bridget muttered. "Certainly not taking a class from Devon."

"Why's that?" Molly inquired, watching as the man worked his way through the crowd, moving against the grain. He looked somewhat familiar, as if she'd seen him around town.

"He owns a candy shop," Bridget said. "Tully's Treats."

"Oh yes, I've been there," Molly said. She'd tried the place when she first moved to town but hadn't been very impressed with the selection, although a few things were good. She refrained from sharing that right now, in public.

Blane edged his way into the classroom, where he joined Devon and Dr. Dunbar, still standing near the doorway. Judging by the frowns on all three faces, none of them were happy to be together. So why had Blane come to Devon's class?

"How's school going so far this semester?" Laura asked Bridget.

"It's a mixed bag," Bridget admitted. "I'm taking advanced forensics, which I love. Chemistry, which is challenging but okay. And Senior English." She groaned. "With Dr. Pryde."

The Bakehouse Three exchanged glances. As relative newcomers to town without many ties to the college, they weren't familiar with the faculty.

"Is he tough?" Molly asked.

"That's an understatement," Bridget said. "I normally love English, but he's super picky about our papers. I'm working on a big one right now." She laughed. "Generations of Superior Bay students have endured his class. We need it to graduate."

"So he's been around for a while?" Carol guessed. "I had a few instructors like that myself. Once they get tenure, they seem to build a reputation for being extra tough." She shared a reminiscent laugh with Molly and Laura, who'd had similar experiences.

The young woman assisting Devon popped out into the hallway. "We're ready to begin," she called over the hum of voices. "Please come back in."

People tossed empty coffee cups and crumpled napkins in the garbage can near the door as they filtered back into the classroom. Molly noticed that Blane and Dr. Dunbar had taken seats at the rear of the room, as onlookers rather than participants.

Cole moved into place again behind the camera, and at the assistant's signal, Devon swung into action. "Welcome back," he said brightly. "In this section of the class, you're going to try your hand at the key technique involved in making chocolate candies—tempering."

The words had barely left his mouth when a heavy gust of wind battered the building, sending a spray of snow against the windows. The lights flickered once, then twice. The students groaned.

Devon frowned anxiously at the ceiling. "I hope we don't lose power."

"If it does go out, the emergency lights will come on," Dr. Dunbar said. "We'll be able to exit, at least."

Molly sighed in resignation. Power outages were always a possibility in the Upper Peninsula, especially during a winter storm. She'd experienced more than her share.

"And class will be over." Devon sounded glum. "But let's cross our fingers and keep going." He held up a hairnet. "Before we handle food, please put one of these on."

After everyone put on the hairnets, joking and mugging for the camera, Devon demonstrated how to chop chocolate for tempering as the students copied his movements. He explained that tempering stabilizes cocoa butter so the finished product would be smooth with a nice texture.

"In a shop, we use special equipment, and you can use a microwave at home," he said. "For the sake of simplicity tonight, though, we're going to temper with a double boiler. In professional applications, steam and water have the potential for disaster, seizing the chocolate. But we're only doing small batches, so if we need to start over, we will."

Molly was glad to have experienced cooks at her table. "Are you two going to help me?" she asked Carol and Laura. "I'd hate to have my chocolate seize up."

"I'll be happy to, if necessary," Laura said. "It's happened to me, and it is not pretty. It turns into a hard, grainy lump."

Each station was set up with a hot plate, a stainless steel pan partially filled with water, and a glass bowl. Under Devon's instruction, Molly heated the water, then suspended the glass bowl in the pan to melt the chopped chocolate.

Every minute or so she stirred, the goal being to melt any lumps. Laura walked over and peered at Molly's chocolate, then checked the candy thermometer clipped to the bowl. "You're doing a great job. This is spot-on."

"Once your chocolate is melted," Devon said, "we're going to seed it with the rest of the chopped pieces, bit by bit. You don't want to move too fast during this step or else the fat will bloom, or separate at the wrong time and cause problems. Stop adding when you bring the mix down to the right temperature, between eighty-eight and ninety degrees since we're using dark chocolate. If there's some left over, that's okay."

Molly's batch was right at ninety degrees when a huge gust of wind hit the building. A loud thud sounded right outside, heavy enough to shake the walls.

"What was that?" someone called out in a frightened voice.

The overhead lights flickered and went out, and a few people screamed.

"Calm down," Dr. Dunbar commanded. The red glow of the emergency lights provided barely enough illumination to see her stern expression. "I think a tree fell."

"A tree? It must have been huge," another student said. "Let's go check it out." She hurried toward the coatrack, followed by others.

"Hold on," Dr. Dunbar called out. "Don't go out there." But the students didn't listen.

"Want to go see what's happening?" Carol asked her friends.

"Why not?" Molly said, switching off her hot plate so it wouldn't still be on when the power returned. "I think class is over for tonight." She gave her perfectly tempered chocolate a rueful glance. "I hope I can replicate that tomorrow."

"Practice makes perfect," Laura said. "You'll get a feel for it."

The foursome removed their aprons and hairnets, grabbed their coats, and filed down the hallway with the others on their way outside. The wind was fierce, blowing gusts of heavy snow right into their faces. With exclamations of dismay, people bent their heads and trudged around the building to where a massive maple lay, tangled roots aloft.

Bridget switched on her phone's flashlight, playing the light across the fallen tree. When the passing beam caught something white gleaming amid the dark earth, she gasped. "What is that?"

Molly waded through a snowbank toward the tree, causing clumps of snow to fall into her boots. Intent on getting a better view, she ignored the discomfort.

"It looks like a skull," Molly said, her heart lurching with horror. "Someone is buried under there."

2

"Buried? You mean a body?" a woman cried out.

Molly scanned the group huddled together in the storm, faces hidden by hoods and hunched shoulders. "I think so, but I'm not totally sure. We need to see it closer."

No one volunteered for this task. Even Devon, Blane, and the camera operator were hanging back, instead of taking charge as many men liked to do.

Carol slid her gloved hand around Molly's arm. "I guess it's up to us."

"We need to keep our distance, though," Laura warned, a shudder in her voice. "Just in case."

Bridget took the lead, her brave light leading the way. "Exactly right. We were talking about crime scene management in class last week."

Crime scene? A chill ran down Molly's spine. Had they stumbled across another murder? Since moving to Loch Mallaig, she and her friends had found themselves involved in one case after another. This time, they'd been innocently making chocolate when a huge tree came down—one with a body hidden among the roots, it appeared.

Because the closer Molly got, the more she saw that the object was unmistakably a skull. She halted and fumbled in her pocket for her phone. "We've seen enough. I'm calling 911."

Molly's words rippled through the crowd, creating a buzz of confusion and curiosity. She tried to tune them out as the call went through.

"Please state your name. And what's your emergency?" an unfamiliar female voice asked. Molly didn't know the night dispatcher.

"If it's a power outage, believe me, we know."

"Molly Ferris. And yes, we've lost power at Superior Bay College." She had to put one hand to her free ear to block the howling wind. "A big tree came down, thankfully not hitting the building. But when it did . . ." She swallowed. "It exposed a skeleton. It might have been there for years, if not decades."

"A skeleton?" The dispatcher's tone was wary. "An animal?"

"No. I'm afraid not." Molly closed her eyes against the horrible sight still etched in her mind. "Chief Thomson knows me well and he'll believe me."

The dispatcher didn't argue further. "We'll send a car right out. It might take a few minutes, though. We've had a lot of calls tonight."

Over by the building, Dr. Dunbar was herding the students away with the help of Devon and Blane. It was a good move, since they would only be in the way if they stuck around. This death was far too old for them to be considered witnesses.

"I understand," Molly replied. "We'll be in room 114 of MacArthur Hall." It was too stormy to stand out here and wait. At least they could keep vigil inside the classroom since the windows overlooked the scene. Perhaps they could put a light out here to mark the spot before the fast-falling snow filled in the exposed hollow under the tree.

When Molly returned her gaze to the fallen tree, Bridget was about three feet away from the skeleton, bent over with her phone. Carol and Laura were standing next to her.

"Bridget," Molly called, trudging as fast as she was able through the deep, dense snow. "What are you doing?"

"See that?" Bridget asked, unperturbed by Molly's abrupt question. She moved the beam, revealing a gleam of silver. "That's a Superior Bay College key chain." She snapped a picture before showing them the enlargement. "You can tell by the pattern."

Although the object was crusted with dirt, Molly could discern the familiar Superior Bay College emblem done in blue and red enamel paint on the silver base. That might answer one question. Unless a key chain had ended up in the ground next to a body after the fact, the crime could be dated to after the college's founding.

"Good clue, Bridget," Molly said. "Make sure you tell the police about it." She scanned the area. The students were gone, but Dr. Dunbar was stomping through the snow toward them.

"Did you get ahold of the police?" she barked at Molly.

"I did, and they'll be here as quick as they can," Molly said, keeping her tone level. No doubt Dr. Dunbar was feeling the weight of responsibility around this event. "Can we get some kind of light to mark the spot? And a tarp to cover the body?" She glanced up at the sky and the flakes still bucketing down. "If we don't do that, it will be buried in snow by the time the police arrive."

Dr. Dunbar gave a grudging nod. "I'll see what we can rustle up."

"We'll be waiting in the classroom," Molly said. "I want to talk to the police when they get here."

"Why?" Dr. Dunbar asked. "Surely they can take it from here."

They could and would, but Molly was still reluctant to leave. "We've worked with the police before," she said. "Chief Thomson knows we're good witnesses."

Dr. Dunbar rocked back on her heels. "You've worked with the police?" She crossed her arms. "What are you, private investigators or something?"

"No, we run a bakehouse." Molly indicated her partners. "Bridget works for us, and she's also a student here." Bridget opened her mouth and, guessing she was going to mention the key chain, Molly gave her a subtle headshake.

"For some reason or another, we tend to get involved with solving crimes," Carol said. "And it's happened again, apparently."

Dr. Dunbar frowned toward the downed tree. "You think it was foul play?"

"What else could it be?" Laura asked. "There's a skeleton buried under a tree."

The professor continued to study the site, teeth worrying at her bottom lip. Then she turned abruptly. "I'm heading back inside for a spotlight and a tarp. Are you coming?"

On the way in, they met Blane Tully coming out. He greeted them with a nod. "I'm leaving," he told Dr. Dunbar as he continued walking. "No point in hanging around."

"See you later, Blane," Dr. Dunbar called after him. "Thanks for coming by." Her voice held the sweetest tone Molly had yet heard from the gruff professor. Maybe Blane didn't annoy her the way Molly and everyone else seemed to.

The corridor was eerie under the dull red glow of emergency lights, and although it was far warmer than outside, Molly fancied she could already feel a chill creeping through the walls. It wouldn't take long now that the heat was out.

In the classroom, Devon's assistant stood at the front of the room, staring with displeasure at the workstations still littered with equipment, dirty utensils, and fragments of chocolate. "And who gets to clean up this mess?" she grumbled. "Three guesses." She jabbed a thumb toward her chest.

"Oh, lighten up, Robina," Devon said. The chocolate star was leaning against the front table, ankles crossed and arms folded. "It won't take long."

"Says the person who doesn't have to do it." Robina pushed a cart forward and began loading used dishes on it.

"Leave it," Dr. Dunbar said. "You can't work in the dark. I'll get some students from the culinary program to help you tomorrow morning. They can run everything through the dishwasher."

The camera operator was putting away his equipment. "What a shame about the power going out. Everything was going so well." He coiled some wires. "Got some great shots of the class."

Devon straightened, his interest caught. "Want to go through the footage back at the resort? Assuming they still have power."

"If you're staying at Castleglen, they have backup generators," Molly said. At his surprised expression, she added, "I know the owner very well."

Understanding dawned on Devon's face. "The special man in your life?"

"Good guess," Molly said with a laugh. Speaking of Fergus, he should be along soon. She'd grabbed a ride to the class with Carol, and Fergus was going to take her home. With their busy schedules, they had to be flexible about spending time together. Not that it mattered to Molly. She loved every moment she could get with him.

While the Bakehouse Three plus Bridget waited, they watched Dr. Dunbar and a janitor she'd found set up a spotlight outside near the tree. The maintenance man also spread out a long tarp, gently covering the body as if tucking it into bed.

In the distance, flashing lights announced the arrival of the police. A rush of relief went through Molly. Soon they'd be able to hand off responsibility for the poor skeleton to Loch Mallaig law enforcement. The local force would have the sad task of excavating the body and identifying the remains, then informing relatives and figuring out who had buried the victim on the college grounds.

Molly prayed that answers would come swiftly and justice would be served. She also sent up a prayer of gratitude that a grieving family would be able to put a loved one to rest.

The outer door in the hall opened, followed by the sound of voices. One stood out clearly above the babble—Fergus. Molly's heart leaped with joy.

"We're gathered in the classroom up here," Dr. Dunbar was saying as footsteps sounded in the hall. "Molly Ferris placed the call."

The professor, Chief Owen Thomson, Officer Greer Anderson, and Fergus entered the room. "Too bad the power's out," the tall, hazel-eyed chief said. "That's going to hamper things."

"We'll have to call in some generators," blonde, athletic Officer Anderson said, then sighed. "And doing forensics in a snowstorm? It couldn't get much more difficult."

Fergus spotted Molly and gave her a wave. She edged around the officers, who were now being introduced to Devon and his team, and ran into his arms. "I'm so glad you're here," she whispered. Tears of shock and sorrow burned in her eyes. "We found a skeleton under a tree that fell down in the storm."

He hugged her tightly, his embrace warm and comforting. "I heard. How terrible." After releasing his grip, he kept an arm around her shoulders. "Ready to go home?"

"Am I ever." Molly gave a little laugh. She couldn't wait to get back to her apartment above the bakehouse and see her sweet Scottie, Angus. "But first I need to talk to Chief Thomson. Oh, and Bridget found a clue."

"Already?" Fergus shook his head. "Why am I surprised? She's been learning from the best."

Molly smacked him lightly. "I never get involved on purpose."

"I know that." Fergus pulled her close and teased, "It's your special talent."

"I'm glad you think so." Molly laughed again, noticing that the tension in her chest had eased. Being with Fergus automatically made her feel better, as if she could face anything with him by her side. And although life in Loch Mallaig was grand, challenging times seemed to abound, at least for Molly.

While Officer Anderson interviewed Devon and his companions, Chief Thomson made his way over to Molly, who had rejoined her friends. "What a night," he said, greeting them with a nod. "Power's out all over except for a few blocks downtown. Your bakery is all right."

"What a relief," Laura said. "Molly could have stayed with one of us, but I was worried about the perishables. Thanks for letting us know."

"I understand you made quite a discovery tonight," Thomson went on. "Tell me what happened."

Molly and the others explained the sequence of events. "Most of us went outside to check out the tree," Molly said after detailing its thunderous fall. "And that's when we saw the skeleton." When she said these words, Fergus gave her shoulders an encouraging squeeze.

"At first we weren't sure what it was," Carol said. "But we knew it was strange."

Molly swallowed at the memory. "That's when we realized we'd better call 911."

"Molly kept us a good distance away," Bridget said. "But I did manage to get a photograph of something interesting."

Chief Thomson raised one brow in disapproval, but instead of scolding the young woman, he asked, "What was it?"

Bridget brought up the photograph on her phone and showed it to him. "This key chain was under there. It's got the Superior Bay logo."

Behind them, Dr. Dunbar gasped, then said, "Sorry to interrupt, but I wanted to let you know that the forensics team has arrived."

Bridget groaned. "I wish I could watch them work. Even if it is snowing like crazy out there."

When Chief Thomson gave her a funny look, she said, "I'm taking advanced forensics this semester. I'm going into forensic science as a career."

The chief sighed, shifting his feet. "I wish I could, Bridget, and perhaps you can get an internship. But right now—"

"I get it," Bridget said without resentment. "I'm only a civilian."

Chief Thomson glanced through the window at the crime scene, obviously anxious to move forward with the investigation. "That's all for now, ladies," he said. "Feel free to head home." He strode away, Dr. Dunbar at his heels. Officer Anderson had already left the room to greet the forensics team.

Robina approached them and announced, "We need to secure this room."

Molly and the others got the hint. They gathered their bags and belongings and left the classroom as a group.

"What a night," Carol said as they trooped down the hallway. "From chocolate to murder."

"I wonder who that poor person is," Laura said. "Bridget, did you ever hear of any missing students or teachers around here?"

"I think I did, once," Bridget said. "You know how college students talk." She trailed behind, fingers busy on her phone. A moment later, she cried, "Aha! I think I have something." She paused. "Or not."

Everyone stopped walking. "Tell us, Bridget," Molly urged. "It's got to be more than we know now."

"Okay, here we go," Bridget said. "A student named Marla Bannerman supposedly drowned in the lake eleven years ago."

"Drowned?" Carol repeated, her tone confused. "That's certainly not the cause of death here."

"Unless she drowned and someone buried her," Molly amended. But even the best forensics team wouldn't be able to prove that from a skeleton. Unless a bone was broken or a weapon found, a bullet or arrow tip for example, it could be almost impossible to determine cause of death for a skeleton.

"Hold on." Bridget was still scanning the site. "She disappeared and they never found a body. I'm guessing that's why they think she went into the water."

"I remember hearing about that too," Fergus said, which wasn't surprising since he had lived in Loch Mallaig all his life. "Such a tragedy. She was barely twenty."

"How devastating." Molly couldn't help but think of her own daughter, Chloe, a twentysomething veterinarian in Milwaukee.

"Very," Laura said. "And you could be right, Bridget. Maybe it is Marla under that tree and they were wrong about her drowning. But we don't even know yet if the person is male or female, or their age."

"You're right," Bridget said, her face glowing with excitement. "Isn't it cool that they can get so much information from a skeleton? In addition to gender and age, they can find out when they lived, their diet, if they had certain diseases and previous broken bones."

"That is amazing," Fergus agreed. He pushed the door open, holding it so they could exit. "I think you've found your passion in life, Bridget." Fergus was fond of Bridget, having gotten to know her well since she was good friends with his son, Neil, who worked in management at Castleglen.

"Me too," she said happily, sailing through the doorway into the snowstorm.

The Range Rover's windshield wipers provided a steady beat as Fergus drove Molly home from Superior Bay College. Molly sat huddled in the passenger seat, staring out into the swirling snowflakes.

Without taking his eyes off the slippery, snow-covered road, Fergus asked, "Doing okay over there?"

"Not really," she admitted, realizing she was still in shock. "I can't wrap my mind around it yet."

"Totally understandable." His voice was soothing. "I'll have you home soon."

"Thanks, Fergus," she said. "I'm glad I'm not driving tonight." Although Molly had driven in her share of snowstorms, she preferred not to, especially at night.

"Anytime, my dear," he said with a tip of his head. "Fergus MacGregor at your service."

That made her laugh, as he had no doubt intended. She forced her mind away from the night's sad discovery. "On another topic, did you and Neil sign up for the iceboat races?"

Fergus grinned. "We sure did. Fortunately, this storm won't amount to much, even if it seems wild right now." A team of volunteers had been meticulously keeping the racecourse on Loch Mallaig's namesake lake clear of snow all season.

"I can't wait to watch you race," Molly said, although she had some trepidation. Iceboats whizzed along at highway speeds. "My sport is much more boring."

Fergus threw her a smile. "Snowshoeing is a challenge in its own right."

"True." Molly laughed. "I'm used to ambling along on my snowshoes, not running." But she'd wanted to participate in the outdoor events beyond being a spectator, fun as that was. Since she couldn't operate a snowmobile, dogsled, or iceboat, and she was pretty uncoordinated on cross-country skis, snowshoeing had been her only option.

"I'll be there to cheer you on," Fergus said. "What time does it start?"

Molly brought up the faire schedule on her phone and gave him the particulars. "What a great lineup," she said, glancing over the list.

Besides the races, the schedule offered an ice sculpture contest, a skating exhibition by local dance troupe The Leaping Lowlanders, various games, vendor booths, and lots of delicious food. The capstone event was a formal Valentine's Day dance at King's Heid Pub, Castleglen's upscale dinner restaurant, which Molly was attending with Fergus.

"The Winter Faire is a big draw this year," Fergus said. "The resort is almost fully booked."

"Good news," Molly said. "I'm sure Bread on Arrival will be busy too." Many of the activities were being held in Dumfries Park, right behind the bakehouse. As they'd experienced during past events, visitors loved exploring the town's quaint shops and eateries.

When they approached downtown, Molly saw to her relief that the electricity was on, as Chief Thomson had said. Streetlamps glowed along the sidewalks and bright windows provided a note of cheer in the dark winter night.

"Here we are." Fergus steered into Bread on Arrival's drive. The bakehouse was located in a former funeral home—a pale yellow Victorian complete with turret, gabled roofs, and gingerbread trim—which had inspired its name.

A few lights twinkled downstairs in the bakehouse, and the silhouette of a dark head with pointed ears was visible in a window upstairs in Molly's apartment. Molly usually left a lamp on for Angus so he wouldn't feel so lonely without her there.

"The welcoming committee knows I'm home." Molly indicated the window as she and Fergus got out of the Range Rover. Their plan was to enjoy a hot drink while watching a favorite television show. Not the most exciting date, but wonderful all the same.

Inside the second-floor apartment, Molly greeted Angus with pats and ear scratches. Then, while Fergus took over, she moved toward the kitchenette. "Coffee, tea, or hot cocoa?" she asked.

"Hot cocoa sounds great, thanks," Fergus said. With Angus tucked under one arm, he switched on the television and settled on the sofa.

Molly filled two mugs with cocoa and topped them with marshmallows. The mugs went on a tray with a plate of snickerdoodles and napkins.

"I'll never view cocoa the same way again," Molly said as she set down the tray on the coffee table.

"Why's that?" Fergus's blue eyes lit up when he noticed the cookies. "Those look good."

"They are. Laura made them." Molly sat on the sofa. Angus, who loved to be the center of attention, curled up between them. "Back to your question. Devon explained how cacao beans are processed and that, at a certain stage, they either become cocoa powder or chocolate."

"I didn't know that," Fergus said. "It's interesting. Oh, the show is on."

They sat companionably in the warm room, sipping cocoa and watching the show, Angus snorting and snuffling as he napped. Outside, the wind continued to howl, but gradually the snowflakes thinned and then stopped.

Despite how cozy it all was, however, Molly sensed that Fergus had something on his mind. It wasn't that he was distant, exactly, but he wasn't as relaxed and responsive as usual. A couple of times, he didn't laugh at a funny line. And Fergus never missed a joke. She thought about asking him what was going on but hesitated. *What if I'm imagining things? Maybe he's tired. Or, more likely, thinking about the resort.*

When the program ended, Fergus stretched with a yawn. "Well, I suppose I'd better get going. I have a long day tomorrow."

"Me too." After switching to a local station for the weather forecast, Molly nudged a sleeping Angus aside and stood.

She was escorting Fergus to the door when a news announcement caught her ear. "Students at a chocolate-making class made a startling discovery tonight," the anchor said.

Molly and Fergus exchanged surprised glances and stopped to listen.

"High winds in the area have caused power outages and downed trees tonight," the newscaster went on, "including at Superior Bay College in Loch Mallaig. The remains of a young female were discovered under a two-hundred-year-old maple that succumbed to a strong gust."

The footage on screen changed to Chief Thomson being interviewed at the scene. The chief's expression was pinched with cold and the seriousness of his report. "The coroner was able to make several determinations pretty quickly," Thomson said, "namely the approximate age and gender of the victim."

"Are there any clues to her identity?" the reporter asked. "Or how she came to be buried there?"

Chief Thomson shook his head. "We'll be following all possible leads. But we do know this—our Jane Doe has a fractured skull. She was a victim of foul play."

3

"Oh, Fergus." Molly found herself wrapped in Fergus's comforting arms again. "How awful."

He kissed the tip of her nose. "I know, sweetheart. The only good news is that the perpetrator will be brought to justice."

Molly looked up at him. "You think? We don't even know for sure how long ago she died. Unless it is Marla Bannerman. But still, that's a pretty cold case."

"I have every confidence that our excellent police force will figure it out." Fergus gave her another squeeze. "Are you okay? I can hang around for a while longer."

Molly stepped back, giving him a gentle push. "No, go on. I'll be fine. It's getting late." Every part of her body ached with weariness, and she knew from experience that if she didn't get enough rest, tomorrow would be difficult to get through.

He shrugged on his coat and after a final kiss, was gone.

Molly wandered back into the den, where she switched off the television and gathered up Angus. His warm bulk felt good in her arms. "Time for bed, sleepyhead."

Soon she was tucked into bed, listening to the wind whistle around the eaves. She thought of the fallen tree and was glad that their Jane Doe was now in out of the cold.

Monday morning, Molly went downstairs as soon as she heard someone else arrive. "Morning," she said as she entered the kitchen and found Laura. "I'll make coffee." She washed her hands and put on an apron.

"Deal," Laura said, tying on an apron. "I'll get going on the Valentine scones as soon as I find the heart-shaped cutter."

"Oh, that's right." Molly plopped a filter into the basket. "Are you doing the strawberry scones again this year?"

"Actually, I thought we should branch out," Laura said. "I want to try a whole range of romantic flavor combinations."

Molly poured water into the coffee maker. "That sounds amazing. What flavor are you making today?"

Laura sifted dry ingredients into a big bowl. "Raspberry and white chocolate. Tomorrow will be chocolate with cranberries. After that, I'm not sure. I'm creating flavors on the fly."

"And you do it so well." Anticipating that Carol would arrive soon, Molly readied three mugs, sugar, and milk.

Molly was pouring the coffee when the back door opened and Carol bustled in. "Hello, hello," Carol sang out. "Is that fresh-brewed coffee I smell?"

"The freshest." Molly topped off the third cup.

Carol traded snow boots for work shoes and hung her parka, then brushed her hair into place. "We had a tree fall down right across our road last night."

"Oh no," Laura said. "I was worried about that this morning. Some trees around me came down too, but thankfully they fell in the woods."

Still tying her apron, Carol bustled across the floor toward the coffee area. "I was annoyed, but Harvey was in his element. He had a chance to fire up his brand-new chain saw."

"A new chain saw?" Molly's brows rose. "Oh my. He really is getting into country life."

"Yes, he is." Carol doctored her coffee. "Fortunately, he had help with the tree. It was pretty big. The road crew was chipping the branches when I went by."

"They'll be doing a lot of that today, sounds like." Molly couldn't help but think of the tree at the college. Not that she'd forgotten. Thoughts of the dead girl hovered in the back of her mind pretty much constantly.

A sad silence fell over the kitchen, and Molly guessed her friends were also thinking about Jane Doe. Laura confirmed it when she asked, "Did you see the news last night?"

"Sure did," Carol said. "Harvey and I usually try to catch the weather before bed. I was kind of surprised to tell the truth. That was pretty fast work on the part of the police and the news team."

"They were probably already here covering the storm," Laura said. "The UP was hardest hit." Her expression was wry. "The dead body story is already all over social media."

"I'll bet." Such a shocking story might even go national. Molly finished her coffee, eager to move to her next task, which was checking the front room. "I hope they identify her quickly and figure out what happened to her."

"Me too," Carol said. "It's just too sad." With a shake of her head, she became all business. "What's on tap today, Laura?"

As Laura told Carol about the Valentine scones, Molly walked to the front of the house. This was a large, yet cozy room furnished with Celtic Northwoods tables and chairs, with wood-and-glass display cases fronting the service counter.

After getting the cash register set up, Molly checked the supply of dishes and paper goods and took an inventory of the cases. She rearranged some items and wrapped others for discounted sale. She set coffee urns to brew and made sure the tea water was hot.

The final task before switching on the rest of the lights was lighting the gas fireplace in the corner. Especially on cold days like this, a flickering fire added the perfect note of welcome and comfort. Once that was done, Molly unlocked the door and flipped the sign in the window. Bread on Arrival was open for business.

Bridget emerged from the kitchen carrying a pan of fresh scones. "Good morning, Molly. How are you today?"

"Fine, thank you." Molly remembered the victim under the tree. "Well, mostly."

Her young employee began loading scones into the case, her expression troubled. "It's so sad. I really think it is Marla, mostly because of the skeleton's vital statistics and the college key chain."

"It seems to fit." Molly peeked out into the parking lot. No customers yet. She circled behind the counter. "I hope they figure out who buried her there."

"Me too," Bridget said. "I researched her disappearance last night. As a college student, I can log into the library's subscription databases. It didn't take long to find articles from back then."

"What did they say?" Molly noticed that Bridget had finished unloading the tray of scones. After another glance into the empty parking lot, she said, "Hold on. Let's talk in the kitchen." The bell above the front door would let them know when customers arrived.

"Sure," Bridget agreed, following Molly into the kitchen.

"Bridget has some info for us," Molly announced to Laura and Carol as she poured coffee for Bridget and refilled everyone else's mugs. It was a good time to chat, because Laura was piping filling into cream puffs and Carol was kneading bread dough.

Bridget leaned against a counter, cradling her mug. "Like I told

Molly, I can log into newspaper and legal databases through the college library. Last night, I checked into Marla Bannerman."

"The college student who disappeared?" Carol asked. She shaped the dough into a ball and plopped it into a bowl to rise under a tea towel.

Bridget nodded. "She was missing, presumed drowned. One of the college skiffs was found capsized in the loch. They thought it was an accident at first, but then rumors circulated that Marla was cheating in school. Plus people said she was 'unstable.'" She bracketed the last word with her fingers.

"So they assumed suicide." Laura grimaced. "But all the while, she was under that tree."

"And if it hadn't fallen down, no one would ever have known," Molly said in a low voice.

"Someone must be freaking out right about now," Bridget said. "Cat's out of the bag. Hopefully they'll make a mistake. Or confess."

"Were you able to find out who her closest friends were?" Carol asked.

"Uh-huh. And you'll never believe who they are." Bridget paused dramatically. "Devon, Blane, Cole, and Dr. Dunbar. Although she wasn't a doctor then, just plain Brianne Dunbar."

"And now they're all together again," Molly mused. "How convenient for the police."

"Blane and Dr. Dunbar never left the area," Bridget said. "And Dr. Dunbar invited Devon to do the class. As for Cole, he's been working with Devon since he started filming videos in his chocolate shop. The right people noticed, and now Devon's a cable star."

"You really learned a lot," Carol said, her tone marveling. "You're a great researcher."

Bridget's smile was modest. "This year's classwork has really honed my skills."

The bell above the bakehouse entrance jingled. "That's my cue," Molly said, pushing through the kitchen door.

She stopped dead in her tracks. Dr. Brianne Dunbar and Devon Macintosh were the first customers of the day.

After a moment, Molly shook off her surprise. "Good morning," she called. "Welcome to Bread on Arrival."

"Good morning to you." Dr. Dunbar unwound a scarf from around her neck, then shrugged out of her wool coat and hung both on the rack.

Devon hung up his coat as well. Swiping a hand through his hair, he grinned at Molly. "Nice place you have here, Molly Ferris."

Molly's heart fluttered. A cable star was complimenting their business—and he knew her name. "Thank you," she said lightly. "It's a lot of work, but we love it."

Devon studied the pastry cases. "Hmm. How do I choose?"

"Those look good." Dr. Dunbar pointed to the heart-shaped scones.

"Raspberry and white chocolate," Molly said, plucking a serving tissue out of the box. "First in our Valentine's Day series."

Devon gave his companion a gentle elbow. "You should definitely get that one."

Dr. Dunbar's complexion pinked, but she set her mouth in a firm line. "What are you talking about?" She folded her arms. "This is a business meeting, Devon."

He appeared wounded. "True. But there's nothing that says we can't have some fun."

"Fun?" Dr. Dunbar raised a brow. "That's hardly appropriate under the circumstances, don't you think?"

Molly's ears perked up. *What circumstances? The discovery of Marla Bannerman's body? Or something else?* Pretending not to notice the tension between the pair, she waited for them to make a decision.

"I'll have a Scottish snowball," Devon said in a subdued tone, his shoulders hunched. His buoyant mood had fled.

"Great choice," Molly said, putting the coconut-covered treat on a plate. "As you can tell, we specialize in Scottish baked goods, as befits Loch Mallaig's heritage. Plus, they're fantastic."

"Cute idea." Dr. Dunbar gave her a slight smile. "I'll take the raspberry and white chocolate. I can't resist. And a medium hot chocolate."

"A large house coffee for me, please," Devon said. "Black."

Bridget entered from the kitchen, her mouth dropping open when she saw Devon and Dr. Dunbar. "Hello," she said. "Thanks for coming by."

Dr. Dunbar squinted at Bridget as if not sure who she was, but Devon smiled. "You're in my class."

Bridget smoothed her apron as she moved forward. "Yes. I'm Bridget Ross." She gave Dr. Dunbar a sideways glance. "I'm also a senior at Superior Bay College." Molly could tell Bridget was dying to question them about Marla Bannerman, but she managed to restrain herself.

"Want to ring this up?" Molly asked Bridget. "I'll get the drinks."

The pair gathered their order and moved to a table near the fireplace. Then, as often happened, the floodgates opened and customers poured in. For the next half hour or so, Molly was busy filling orders, stocking the bakery cases, and cleaning tables. Bridget was right behind her, knowing exactly what to do next as she always did.

During a lull, Molly noticed Dr. Dunbar and Devon, who sat with heads close together, talking in low tones. Neither seemed happy. She couldn't blame them. The discovery that a close friend had likely been murdered would upset anyone.

An official determination of the skeleton's identity had yet to be made, but Molly had the feeling that Bridget was right. After all, how many Superior Bay students or staff had gone missing while at school?

"Lost in the clouds, are ye, my dear Molly?" a voice with a soft Scottish burr asked.

Startled out of her thoughts, Molly turned to see Alastair Thomson, Chief Thomson's father, standing at the counter. She'd been so preoccupied that she hadn't noticed him come in.

"Sorry, Alastair," Molly said. "What can I get you?"

Rubbing his thick, white mustache, Alastair studied the bakery case with sharp blue eyes. A retired tax attorney, Alastair now devoted much of his time to leading The Piping Yoopers, a local bagpiper troupe. Molly and Fergus were members, along with Officer Greer Anderson and a dozen or so others.

Alastair settled on a cinnamon scone and a large tea. Before he left the counter, he said, "There's something I've been meaning to tell ye."

Molly smiled. One of the best things about running the bakehouse was seeing local friends and acquaintances on a regular basis. "What's that, Alastair?"

"I assume you heard that The Leaping Lowlanders are doing a skating exhibition?" He barked a laugh. "Scottish reels on ice skates, can you imagine?"

Molly pictured herself taking part in the event. "If it were me, it would be called flailing on ice." She and Alastair shared a laugh.

"So," Alastair said. "Dallis Witherspoon gave me a call. He had planned to use recorded music, but now he'd like the Yoopers to play." His expression was sheepish. "I told him yes."

"We've played for them plenty of times before," Molly said. "I was planning to attend anyway, so I'll be happy to play."

"That's great, lass." Alastair beamed. "Your playing has come such a long way. Ye should be mighty proud of yourself."

Molly blushed. "It'll be a fun way to participate in the faire."

"I'll get the set list to you later today," he said.

As he ambled off to find a table, Molly noticed that Dr. Dunbar was sitting alone at the table by the fire. A quick glance at the coatrack confirmed that Devon's coat was gone. He must have slipped out while Molly was talking to Alastair.

Dr. Dunbar reached for a discarded newspaper at the adjacent table. After straightening it out, she skimmed the front page.

And burst into tears.

4

Without hesitation, Molly grabbed a box of tissues and hurried across the bakehouse floor to Dr. Dunbar's table. So far, Molly had found the professor to be aloof, even cold. Right now, though, she was a fellow human in distress, and Molly's heart went out to her.

"Here you go," Molly said, setting the tissues within reach. "Do you want to talk?" She was prepared to leave Dr. Dunbar in peace if that was what the woman wanted.

Dr. Dunbar plucked a tissue from the box and dabbed her eyes. "I could use a friend right now," she said in a wavering voice.

Molly pulled out a chair and perched on it, allowing Dr. Dunbar to lead the conversation. Bridget was clearing a table nearby and edged closer in curiosity. At Molly's nod, she sat on the other side of the professor.

"Did you hear the latest?" Dr. Dunbar stabbed a finger at the newspaper headline, which announced the skeleton's discovery. "I just got a news alert. It's Marla, like we thought. Seeing her death on the front page is so awful. It's right in my face."

Bridget's mouth opened, but Molly silenced her with a significant look. "And who was Marla to you?" Molly asked Dr. Dunbar in a gentle tone.

Dr. Dunbar sniffed. "She was my roommate. She killed herself during our senior year. Or at least that's what everyone thought."

"How terrible," Molly said, and she meant it. The loss of a young person was always tragic. All that potential, gone in an instant.

"Yes." Dr. Dunbar blew her nose. "We thought she'd gone out on the lake and jumped overboard. The boat was capsized and drifting. Such a simple explanation, right?"

"Sounds like one." Molly's pulse beat faster. "But you think it was staged?" She was quickly coming to that conclusion herself.

Dr. Dunbar shrugged. "Possibly. But Marla might have fallen out and then been attacked on shore." She swallowed visibly.

"Attacked by whom?" Molly held her breath waiting for the answer. What would Chief Thomson think if she cracked the case right here, in the bakehouse?

Head bent, the professor picked at the hem of her sweater. "There was a lot going on at the time, and it was over a decade ago. But I do remember Marla being upset."

"About what?" Molly asked.

Across the table, Bridget had been tapping at her phone. She held it up so Molly could see a headline: *Body Identified as Marla Bannerman.* Quick work on the coroner's part. Maybe they'd still had dental records and the like to compare.

"Being a senior is exciting, but stressful." For the first time, Dr. Dunbar seemed to notice Bridget. "You know what I mean, right?"

Bridget nodded. "I sure do. It's both exciting and scary to think about graduating and going out into the world."

The professor's head went down again. "That was definitely part of it for Marla. She was struggling with a couple of classes. And on top of that, she had relationship drama."

Molly raised her eyebrows. Those closest to a victim were most often responsible. That included romantic partners. "Was she involved with someone?"

"Yes and no. She was very popular." Dr. Dunbar sighed as though reluctant to share the information. "All the guys in our circle had crushes on her. Blane. Cole. Devon." She exhaled again. "She also confided in me that she was scared of someone." The tears burst forth again. "To my everlasting shame, I didn't believe her. I thought she was exaggerating."

Molly exchanged a concerned glance with Bridget. "You really need to talk to the police, Dr. Dunbar," Molly said. "You might know something that will help them solve this crime."

The professor's lips twisted. "I'm going to call them. Believe me, I'll tell them everything I know." She pushed back in her chair. "Thanks for being so kind, but now I'd better get going. I have a class to teach."

Molly and Bridget watched as she stumbled across the room, reaching blindly for her coat and tugging it on.

Bridget stood, her gaze fixed on Dr. Dunbar as she left the bakehouse. "Wow," she said. "It's possible that Marla's friends might know something about her death. Or—and I hate to suggest this—they might have been involved."

"It's usually someone close to the victim." Molly rose. "Truly random attacks are rare."

"Yes, we talked about that in class." Bridget began to clear the table, and Molly pitched in. "We also discussed listening to people when they feel threatened. Obviously Dr. Dunbar didn't take Marla's concerns seriously."

Molly's hands stilled. "And she'll have to live with that regret the rest of her life. I sure hope I'd do better if someone came to me."

Bridget smiled at Molly. "You'd identify the problem and deal with it in a snap. The bad guy would be locked up by nightfall."

Her employee's faith warmed Molly's heart. "Oh, Bridget. I'm glad you think so highly of me. I'll try to live up to it." She started toward the kitchen with her stack of dirty dishes, but paused. "Did you see Devon leave? He somehow got by me."

Bridget's eyes were wide. "I sure did. He stormed out of here, but in a quiet way. He was frowning and swinging his arms, so he was clearly mad."

"I wonder if Dr. Dunbar accused him of something."

"She might have," Bridget said. "Or perhaps he was upset about Marla." A light shone in her eyes. "We'll see him at class later tonight. Maybe we can question him."

"Please be careful, Bridget," Molly said, although she was also dying to know Devon's thoughts about Marla. She'd certainly gotten herself in a pickle more than once while investigating, and she didn't want anything to happen to her young friend.

"Of course I'll be careful," Bridget said. "I've learned from the best—you."

Why isn't that comforting? "I'm going to take these dishes to the kitchen." Molly nodded to the front counter, where Carol was now waiting on a big group of new customers. "Can you help Carol?"

"Sure thing," Bridget said, wiping the table down. "After I'm done here."

In the kitchen, Laura was bent over an array of cookbooks plus her table. "Hi," she said to Molly. "I'm working on Valentine ideas."

Molly carried the dishes to the washing area. "Anything to share yet?"

Laura hummed. "I think I can improve the strawberry scones we do every year by making them strawberries and cream scones instead. And how does red velvet sound?"

"They both sound amazing," Molly said. "I bet customers will really get into a wider variety of romantic flavor options."

Laura added to her shopping list. "We'll track how the flavors do and keep the best ones."

Carol burst into the kitchen, her eyes wide. "Did you hear the news? They've confirmed that the skeleton is Marla Bannerman."

"I heard it from Dr. Dunbar a bit ago," Molly admitted. "I hadn't gotten a chance to update you yet."

"No problem." Carol waved that off. "I saw you talking to her while I was waiting on that huge party. Three generations in one family, here for the Winter Faire."

Laura made a final note and set aside her pencil. "All done for now." She squared her shoulders. "Tell us everything, Molly."

Molly found her phone and brought up the news alert, then read it to them. "After Devon left, Dr. Dunbar started crying. I took some tissues over to her table and found out that she'd seen the announcement." Molly relayed their conversation. "I urged her to talk to the police, and she said she would," she concluded.

Carol appeared thoughtful. "Hopefully she knows something that will lead them in the right direction."

"They should talk to Devon, Blane, and Cole too," Laura said. "There might be someone else involved, a person we don't know about."

"Very true," Molly said. "And I'm sure Chief Thomson will get to the bottom of it." The entrance bell jingled. "I'd better get back out front. It's shaping up to be a busy day."

"It will be a busy week with the faire and Valentine's Day coming up," Carol said. "I'm going to catch up on some office work, if that's okay." In addition to baking, former math teacher Carol did the bakehouse accounting.

"No problem," Molly said. "Bridget and I will hold down the fort. And Hamish will be here from noon to three when Bridget leaves for class."

"I'm going to get moving on my second round of baking," Laura said. "Try to get ahead for tomorrow."

"No chance of being bored around here," Molly said as she headed toward the kitchen door. "Even in the dead of winter." And that was a good thing. Molly preferred being busy. At first she'd wondered about living in such a small town after the hustle and bustle of Chicago, where she'd worked as an event planner. Happily, her concerns had proven to be unfounded.

To her surprise, Chief Thomson and Officer Greer Anderson were waiting at the counter while Bridget helped someone else. Both were in uniform.

"Good morning," Molly said. "What can I get you?"

"The largest coffee you have," Greer said with a laugh. "I'm exhausted."

Molly noticed that the officer's pretty hazel eyes were shadowed with fatigue. "Long night?"

Greer nodded. "And it's going to be a long day."

"I'll take a large coffee too," Chief Thomson said. "And a cinnamon scone." He hesitated then said, "Did you hear that we identified the victim?"

"I did," Molly said. "It's tragic. Marla's roommate was in here this morning, quite upset." At their questioning glances, she clarified. "Dr. Brianne Dunbar, from Superior Bay College. She was at the chocolate class last night."

Chief Thomson grunted. Although the Bakehouse Three had helped with many cases, his acceptance of that help stopped short of official endorsement. No matter how insightful, clever, or, as Molly often thought, lucky they were, they were still civilians and amateurs.

"Anyway," Molly went on. *In for a penny, in for a pound, right?* "She told me that she was Marla's roommate when she died and that Marla was scared about something. Or someone."

Now the police would be sure to question Dr. Dunbar, in case she chickened out and didn't call them. Molly suppressed a twinge of guilt about sharing the professor's revelations. If Dr. Dunbar had been more forthcoming eleven years ago, perhaps Marla would still be alive.

Molly flipped the sign to *Closed* promptly at three-thirty, glad that no customers were lingering today. Sometimes they did, and it was the bakehouse policy never to shoo them out or make them feel unwelcome. Today, though, the Winter Faire had drawn them away, with many activities happening in the adjacent Dumfries Park.

As she moved through the room doing the last of the tidying up, her phone pinged with a text. Bridget. *Can the B3 meet me in the library before class? For research purposes.*

Molly guessed what Bridget was referring to—Marla Bannerman. *I can,* she replied in a text. *Let me check with the others.*

Carol and Laura were in the kitchen, preparing to leave. "I'm going to dash home and do some laundry," Laura said. "We've got chocolate class at five-thirty, and then we're meeting the guys at the faire after, right?"

"As far as I know," Carol said. "I plan on hitting Harvey's favorite food truck for dinner tonight."

"The Sausage Guy, right?" Molly waved her phone. "Can we stop by the college library before class? Bridget wants us to help her research the case."

"That's fine," Laura said. "If we all help, we should be able to get a lot done."

"Any plans this afternoon, Molly?" Carol asked as she put on her coat.

"Not really. I need to walk Angus." An idea popped into Molly's mind. "Maybe I should go out to Tully's Treats to buy some candy for my parents and Chloe."

Both Carol and Laura gave her knowing faces. "And do a spot of investigating?" Carol asked with a grin.

"Something like that," Molly admitted. "The thing is, I've had Tully's candy before and I didn't love it. I'm not sure about buying it as a gift. On the other hand, I'm certainly not going to produce enough in class to give to everyone."

"The chocolate is hit or miss there, I noticed," Carol said. "I bought some for Harvey's birthday. You can't go wrong with his mints or his truffles, though."

"Thanks," Molly said. "I'll check those out." She sent a text to Bridget saying that they would all meet her at the library before class, then she shed her apron and went upstairs to see her favorite dog.

After taking Angus for a brisk walk, Molly fed him dinner before hopping into her Honda Fit for the drive to Tully's Treats. The candy store was located on the fringe of downtown, in an older clapboard building painted bland beige. A sign over the front entrance read *Tully's Treats Since 1890* in scrolled black script.

Molly parked in front, avoiding forlorn piles of dirty snow as she made her way to the entrance. She paused to study the display window, which held a miniature model of Loch Mallaig, including the blue loch and the surrounding hills. A little train circling the village held tiny, closed boxes labeled *Tully's Treats*. A cute, low-maintenance idea, easier than displaying actual goods for sale, which had to be rotated or thrown out when they went stale.

Bells over the door jingled when Molly walked into the small shop. Straight ahead was the main counter, with other display cases on either side. Selections included chocolate-covered fruit, truffles, and filled chocolates, including the mint flavor Carol had mentioned. The sweet aroma of chocolate and vanilla clung to the air.

Blane Tully emerged through swinging doors that led to a back room. He was dressed in a spotless apron and a chef's skullcap. "Good afternoon," he said. "How may I help you?" His gaze skipped over

Molly without a hint of recognition. For a man who made his living serving the public, he was less than warm and friendly.

"Hi," she said, moving closer to the cases. "I want to buy some Valentine's gifts for my family." She scanned a menu resting near a pile of assorted-size boxes. "A small box and a medium, please."

"Red boxes?" he asked, sliding on plastic gloves. "With white bows?"

"Perfect." Molly studied the array of truffles, which included raspberry, hazelnut, tiramisu, and orange. "A friend recommended your truffles and mints."

He slid the case open with a gloved hand. "That's nice to hear. Who is your friend? Does she live locally?"

"Carol MacCallan," Molly said, seizing the opportunity to guide the conversation. "And yes, she does. She was at Devon's chocolate class with me last night." When he stared blankly, she added, "We own Bread on Arrival, along with a third friend."

"Oh yes. That's a very clever name, I always think, considering the history of your building."

"Thanks." Molly tried to concentrate on the truffles so she could choose an assortment. Other flavors included chai, lemon, espresso, and salted caramel. "How many pieces in a small box? And medium?"

He gave her the amounts, and she told him which ones she wanted, leaving room for the square mints.

As Blane selected truffles, he asked, "What did you think of the class?"

"It was fascinating," Molly said. "I really enjoyed hearing about the whole process, from bean to bar. Tonight, we're going to try hand dipping."

"It takes years to become an expert," Blane said in a warning tone. "I started when I was a child, and I still make mistakes."

"I only want to make chocolate now and then for my family and friends," Molly said. "I think the point of the class is to give us an overview. And it's fun."

"These are made from family recipes." Blane waved a truffle before slotting it into the box. "My great-great-grandfather came to this country from Scotland, where his family had a sweets shop, as they call it there. We've been in business in this location for over a century."

"That's impressive," Molly said, wondering what he was getting at.

"Did you know that Devon used to work here when he was a teenager?" He went on without waiting for her response. "We were best friends. And because he was my best friend, my parents trusted him." A deep line appeared between his brows. "They even shared our signature family recipes with him."

Now Molly had a good idea where the conversation was headed. Although Blane's voice hadn't risen, a palpable tension had fallen over the room.

"Do you mean Devon stole your recipes?"

"I would never say that in so many words, because it's incredibly hard to prove." Blane gestured with a salted caramel truffle. "Salted caramel is incredibly popular these days. We were among the first to make it in this country. It also happens to be one of Devon's top flavors. Check out his site if you don't believe me."

"I see," Molly muttered as Blane plopped the truffle back on the pile. "I guess it happens in all kinds of industries."

The chocolatier closed Molly's boxes with deft movements. "That doesn't make it sting less. You expect better from a friend."

"Very true," Molly said, feeling she should make some remark but trying to stay neutral. Why had Blane come to Devon's class if he harbored such ill will? Had he planned to confront his former friend? Maybe those plans had been derailed by the discovery of Marla's body.

Blane wrapped the candy boxes with ribbon. "I suppose I should let it go. We have bigger concerns to face right now." Sadness clouded his dull-brown eyes. "I still can't wrap my mind around what happened to Marla." He seemed to assume that Molly knew who Marla was.

"It's tragic," Molly said. "If that tree hadn't blown down, she might never have been found."

He stacked the boxes on the counter by the register and punched numbers into the cash register. "It's a real shocker. I'm going to try to catch up to Cole later, see how he's doing." Molly tilted her head in a silent question, so he added, "Cole Keith, the cameraman. He used to date Marla."

Thinking of the young man's likely distress, Molly's hand flew to her lips. "He must be devastated." Or not—if he had killed her.

"I'm sure. He was pretty head over heels." Blane made a tsk-tsking sound. "Too bad she was about to dump him."

"Really?" Molly was riveted. Then, remembering why she was there, she dug out her wallet. "How do you know?"

"She told me her plan. She had a big crush on Devon. But hey, what's new?" Blane's smile was sour. "Golden boy Devon always wins."

5

A short while later, the Bakehouse Three and Bridget were seated in a corner of Superior Bay College's spacious library. Molly leaned forward across the library table, not wanting to disturb students studying nearby—or allow them to eavesdrop either. "Blane told me Marla was dating Cole, but she wanted to break up with him and date Devon."

Bridget rolled her eyes. "Sounds like college all right." Her face sobered. "And motive for Cole."

"True," Carol said. "But I'm not sure we should trust anything Blane says. He's obviously bitter about Devon's alleged theft."

Laura was busy on her phone. "Not so alleged. Check this out." The screen showed Devon's website, featuring his "famous salted caramel truffles" front and center. She searched a little more. "Those are the candies that first attracted national attention. They were written up in a magazine, and then he went on talk shows as a featured chef."

"If I were Blane and my family invented the recipe, I wouldn't be happy either," Molly had to admit. "He probably thinks he should have gotten all the notoriety. Or at least some credit."

"I can really relate," Laura said. "What if someone stole one of my original recipes and used it to become famous?" Her lips set in a firm line. "We'd have to talk."

"They'd have to talk to all of us," Carol assured her.

"Glad you have my back," Laura said. "The Blane-Devon rivalry is interesting, but we'd better get back to Marla. We don't have much time before class."

They all faced Bridget, who was in charge of the research effort. She gestured toward her open laptop. "I thought we'd search the college and newspaper archives during the time Marla was a student here. I can log in on my laptop, but you'll need to use college computers." She waved to a row of available computers nearby. "They're all logged into the system."

"We can do that," Carol said, starting to rise from her seat.

"Hold on a second," Bridget said, and Carol sat again. "I need to stop by Professor Pryde's office before class and drop off my latest draft. Will you come with me?" They must have appeared confused, because she hurried to add, "Professor Pryde was teaching here when Marla was a student. All students had senior English back then too."

"So he might have some insights into Marla's state of mind," Molly said. "Or know something about her relationships?"

"It's possible," Bridget said. "Leave no stone unturned, right? Oh, and one more thing. Please make note of the sources you investigate, okay? I'm working on a paper about investigative techniques."

"Well, aren't you the clever one?" Carol teased as she stood. "Getting us to help you with your schoolwork."

Bridget's cheeks flushed. "Don't worry, I plan to mention your contributions in my paper. By name."

"I'm teasing." Carol patted Bridget on the shoulder. "Any investigator worth her salt has a team. And we're it."

"You're more than that," Bridget said. "You're my mentors. And an inspiration."

"Oh, Bridget, what a compliment," Molly said, pleased to think that she was having a positive influence on the younger generation.

While Bridget bent over her laptop, the three women settled at the computer bank and brought up the library catalog on their monitors. Molly decided to search the local newspapers for mention of Marla's death. It didn't take long to find the articles. *Student Missing, Feared Drowned,* one headline read. Brianne Dunbar was interviewed in the article and reported that her roommate often rose early and went out rowing on the loch. Brianne didn't think anything of it at the time because she had gone to her own early classes. But then reports of a capsized boat had spread.

Molly read on. Divers were brought in to search, but no sign of Marla had been found. Another article a couple of months later said that she'd been declared dead, presumed by drowning. Sadly, Marla was alone in the world, both her parents and remaining grandparent having passed away during her college years.

To think that all along, Marla had been under the maple tree. Someone had attacked her in the early morning, maybe before dawn, then buried her. And no one had noticed. The tree's position between the loch and the classroom building was probably why. At that time of day, the classrooms were empty. The college dorms and faculty housing were on the other side of the building or a distance away, beyond a copse of woods.

Molly sent the articles to print then asked her friends, "Any luck?"

"I found a retrospective about Marla with quotes from her friends in the school newspaper," Carol said. "I sent that to the printer already."

"How about you?" Molly asked Laura, who was still studying her screen.

"This doesn't mention Marla, but it's interesting." Laura gestured toward the monitor. "What do you think?"

The other two women scooted their chairs closer, and Bridget came over and leaned over Laura's shoulder. Together, they peered at a column in the student publication called *Hints and Innuendo.*

"Nice name," Carol said with a laugh. "That would probably be the first thing I'd read every week."

"It's a college gossip column?" Molly guessed.

"Exactly," Laura said. "It has what are called blind items. No names. People needed to put the clues together for themselves."

"It's not in the newspaper now," Bridget said, her smile wry. "We have social media for all the hints and innuendos we need."

"I'll bet," Molly said.

"What did you find?" Carol asked Laura.

Laura turned back to the page and scrolled. "Listen to this. 'We all know that senior year is tough. But are some students taking shortcuts to make sure they graduate? Naughty, naughty.'"

"So someone was allegedly cheating at their schoolwork," Molly said.

"There is no indication that this involves Marla," Bridget said. "We can't get sidetracked."

Carol nodded. "You're right, Bridget. It may have nothing to do with Marla's life or death. But it is a sign of trouble on campus."

"That's a good point." Bridget jotted something in her spiral notebook. "Can you please print that article, Laura?"

"Of course." Laura sent the pages to the printer, then exited the file. "I found something else interesting in an earlier edition." She brought up another *Hints and Innuendos* column. "Listen to this. 'Campus security interrupted their naps to quell shenanigans at one of the dorms. Three guesses which one. Disciplinary action may follow.' Any thoughts, Bridget?"

Bridget shook her head. "Nothing like that has happened on campus since I've been here. We'll have to do some more digging."

"Again, we don't know if Marla was involved," Laura said. "But it's worthwhile to find out."

"Something obviously went very wrong at the college that year," Molly said. "We need to follow every lead." In past cases, Molly had learned never to jump to quick conclusions. Sometimes the tiniest thread unraveled the entire mystery.

"What did you find, Bridget?" Carol asked. "Any luck?"

"Actually, I was doing something else." Bridget unfolded a double sheet of paper, revealing a map of the campus with hand-drawn notations. "I'm trying to figure out connections and timing by using this map." She tapped an X. "This is where we found Marla." She moved her finger to another X. "And this is where the boat was found drifting." The second spot was a distance away from the classroom building, not far from the docks where kayaks and skiffs were stored.

"Hmm," Laura said. "That makes me wonder if she was ever in the boat at all. You'd think it would have been found closer to the tree."

"I agree," Carol chimed in. "I think someone staged the capsized boat near the docks."

"Sure looks that way." Molly touched the map's edge. "I like seeing it laid out like this—a visual representation of the crime."

"Me too," Bridget said. "I'll keep adding details as we learn them." She checked the wall clock. "Dr. Pryde might be able to help." She sighed. "And maybe talking about Marla will distract him from the shape my paper is in."

After collecting their pages from the printer, the Bakehouse Three trailed along with Bridget to Dr. Pryde's office, located on the second floor in one of the classroom buildings. At this time of day, most of the doors on this floor were closed and the lights off, but Dr. Pryde's door stood ajar.

Murmured voices drifted out. "He's still with somebody," Bridget said as she shifted from foot to foot, her expression anxious. "I can't wait to get this over with."

"He's that tough, huh?" Molly asked with sympathy. Bridget, who certainly didn't lack confidence, seemed intimidated by the man. Thinking back on her own college years, Molly wondered if scaring students was the right approach. It might make them work harder in class, but she doubted it was productive in the long run.

"Yes, he is." Bridget sighed. "Honestly, if the class wasn't a require-ment, I would have dropped it the first week."

While they waited, they paced around a bit, taking in notices on a bulletin board or checking their phones. Molly had a message from Fergus: *Still on for the faire tonight?*

Yes, can't wait, she wrote back. After a pause, she added, *Mind if I bring someone else along?*

Does he have four legs and a handsome face?

Guessed it on the first try, she answered, chuckling. *He could use the outing.* Poor Angus had been cooped up far too much lately. If they were eating outside, then there was no reason they couldn't bring him along. He was a very well-behaved dog.

Fergus sent back a thumbs-up emoji. *I'll meet you and our chaperone at the bakehouse after your class.*

Dr. Pryde's door squeaked open and a young student slipped out, books clasped to her chest. She nodded at Bridget. "You can go in now." She barely glanced at the others before scurrying down the hall.

Bridget exhaled deeply. "Here we go. I'll keep it short. Then, if it's okay with him, I'll call you in. Okay?"

"That's fine," Molly said. "You'll do great," she added with the same tone she had used so many times when Chloe had been nervous.

"Hope so." Bridget pulled a face as she entered the room. But her voice was cheerful as she said, "Good evening, Dr. Pryde. I have my draft for you." She narrowed the door to a crack again.

The trio moved down the hall a short distance, using the time to talk about bakehouse business. They kept their voices low so as not to disturb Bridget and Dr. Pryde. After about ten minutes, Bridget opened the door and waved at them. Molly noticed that she looked relieved. The review of her paper must have gone well.

Dr. Pryde stood as they entered. He was a tall, cadaverous man with horn-rimmed eyeglasses and a mane of white hair. "Nice to meet you," he said in a resonant voice after Bridget made the introductions. "I confess to enjoying far too many of your delectable homemade goodies." He patted his midsection.

"Glad to hear it," Laura said.

Carol squinted at the professor, then smiled. "Large tea with cream and Empire biscuits."

"I am impressed." Dr. Pryde's thick brows rose. "You remembered my favorite order." He gestured toward a line of visitor chairs. "Please, have a seat."

With all five of them in the room, it was pretty snug. His office was small, with bookshelves all around the perimeter and even under the lone window. The one personal touch was a spider plant perched on a shelf above the professor's head, its tendrils dangling. As he sat, one brushed his hair.

Molly hid a smile as she sat on a hard wooden chair. Apparently he didn't like his students to get too comfortable.

Dr. Pryde removed his glasses and swung them by one arm. He leaned back in his chair, rocking gently. "What can I do for you?"

Molly took the lead. "We were there when Marla Bannerman's body was discovered."

The swinging of the glasses paused, and Dr. Pryde sucked in an audible breath. Then he blinked several times and apparently recovered. "Such a tragedy. Marla was one of my most gifted students. In that year and, quite frankly, in the decade since." He gave Bridget a small smile. "Present company excluded."

Bridget perked up, sitting straighter on her chair but didn't speak. Molly was glad for the young woman, especially in light of the anxiety she'd felt over her work in this particular subject.

Dr. Pryde went on in a musing tone. "I'm not sure what career Marla would have chosen, but I hoped she would become a writer. She was a natural—that's the only way to put it. My role was merely to guide her, to make suggestions that strengthened her work." He stared off into space, lost in his memories. "That's why I never understood . . ." His voice trailed off.

"Tell us," Molly urged. "Anything you know might be important in figuring out how she died." What he was hinting at might support the idea that Marla's death was related to problems on campus.

The professor eyed her for a long moment. "What's your role in all this, Mrs. Ferris?" He cast his cool gaze over Carol and Laura as well, as if seeing what they had to say.

"Our role isn't official," Molly said. "But in the past, Chief Thomson has appreciated our help in solving local crimes."

"My friends are very talented investigators," Bridget put in, her voice earnest. "I assure you the police welcome their help."

"And if you can tell us something that sheds light on Marla's death," Molly added smoothly, "we'll pass that along to them and they will take it from there."

Dr. Pryde cleared his throat. "All right then." He folded his hands on his desktop. "What I'm going to tell you must stay here, in this room. With the exception of informing the police, if anything seems relevant." Once they all nodded, he continued. "Marla's last paper was a mess, not even close to her usual standards. And worse, something about it was definitely off." He set his jaw, as if steeling himself for what he had to say next. "I discovered that large portions of it were plagiarized."

"Plagiarized?" Laura repeated. "Is that the scandal the school newspaper was talking about?"

Dr. Pryde nodded, his expression sad. "I usually like to handle these things discreetly—with appropriate consequences, naturally—but

I had a teaching assistant with loose lips. It was all over school before I could contain it."

"That probably contributed to the theory that Marla killed herself," Carol said slowly. "She'd gotten caught cheating."

"I'm afraid you're correct," Dr. Pryde said. "After she disappeared, feared drowned, I'm sorry to say the pieces came together to indicate that. Over the semester, she'd become volatile and erratic, not her usual well-balanced self at all." He frowned. "Not that I saw this in class, but I heard stories afterward."

"She was murdered, Dr. Pryde," Molly said. "She didn't kill herself out of shame over plagiarizing a paper. So unless her behavior contributed to that in some way, it was only a red herring."

The professor laced and unlaced his fingers, considering what Molly had said. "You're right. We made assumptions, put the pieces together in a way that made sense. It's what people do when the unexpected happens." He shook his head. "I tell you, her disappearance rocked the campus. Even her gang of rowdy friends settled down and stopped wreaking havoc."

"Which dorm did Marla live in?" Bridget asked. "I heard one in particular used to get in trouble a lot."

Dr. Pryde smiled in memory. "You're talking about Lakeside. Our biggest dorm and the site of many a party, I'm afraid. Marla lived there."

So that blind item in the school newspaper might also have involved Marla, Molly realized. "Who were her rowdy friends?" she asked. She had a feeling that she would recognize the names, but she wanted to hear them from him.

Dr. Pryde pursed his lips. "The names escape me for the most part, except for a couple. Brianne Dunbar is still with us, as you know, a very well-respected food science professor. But she was a minor player.

The ringleader was Devon Macintosh." He bestowed a faint smile on his audience. "Who would have thought that troublemaker would become a cable television star? Although he certainly has more than his fair share of charisma. I'm fairly certain that's the sole reason he didn't get expelled."

6

After leaving Dr. Pryde's office, Molly paused to peer out a hallway window toward the loch, now shrouded in darkness. To her left was the building where the chocolate-making classes were held, and to her right was a three-story dorm.

"That's Lakeside," Bridget said. "If I didn't live at home, that's where I'd want to stay. The rooms are nice, set up in suites for two or four students."

"And Marla lived there with Dr. Dunbar," Molly said. "A piece of information for your map."

The women continued down the stairs and out into the cold night, striding briskly along the path to the classroom building. Molly recognized some of the other pedestrians going in the same direction as fellow chocolate-making students. She wondered if people would drop out after the discovery of the skeleton—or if most would be even more eager to attend. She suspected it could go either way.

Inside the bustling classroom, students removed coats and donned aprons, chatting amiably. Devon was at the front of the room conferring with Cole and Robina while Blane and Dr. Dunbar stood together in a corner.

"The gang's all here again," Carol murmured.

"I see that," Molly said, setting her bag under the table. Tonight the tempering setup was again in place, but hand mixers and a stack of candy molds had been added to each table.

The volume of chatter fluctuated as everyone got settled.

During a lull, Molly clearly heard Robina's voice. "That is *my* fruit ganache recipe." Other voices rose again, but Molly saw Devon give Robina a placating smile. Then she heard his words, "What does it matter who gets credit?" In response, Robina huffed and turned to Cole, and a moment later, the pair walked off.

Interesting. Molly had only heard a snippet, but she'd been on the receiving end of supervisors taking credit for her work. They often used the tactic of trying to make her feel small for wanting her due. Relief made her sigh as she realized that would never happen again. She and her supportive partners respected each other's contributions.

Cole fiddled with his camera for a couple of minutes while Robina set up lights. Devon gave a piercing whistle that silenced the room. "All right, class," he said with a wicked grin. He rubbed his hands together. "It's time to get to work."

A cheer went up from the crowd, and Cole quickly panned the room to capture the happy faces. Robina had moved off to one side, where she watched the action intently, whispering into a headset similar to one Cole wore.

"Last night we had a bit of an interruption, so today we're going to temper chocolate again." Devon paused. "And make some chocolates the easy way."

The students exchanged glances, wondering what he was talking about.

"The traditional way to make chocolate-covered candy is to hand dip a stiff filling." Devon picked up a pronged fork with a long handle and speared a square from a tray. "This is salted caramel ganache, my signature flavor."

Molly snuck a peek at Blane, remembering he had claimed Devon stole his family recipe. The chocolate shop owner was standing with arms folded and a blank expression, giving nothing away.

Devon went on. "I'm going to give a demonstration, but you'll learn how to dip tomorrow. Today, I'll teach you an easier method."

While they watched, he skillfully dipped the square, finishing with a practiced swirl. He placed the beautiful candy carefully onto plastic wrap to set, then showed them the twisting technique, which made a thicker coating.

"Tricky," Laura muttered.

"Agreed," Molly said with a laugh. "How many pieces will I lose in the chocolate?"

"It definitely requires practice, which is why we're dipping tomorrow," Devon said, making Molly blush. She hadn't realized he could hear her. "But you'll get the hang of it."

After he dipped a few more chocolates, Robina brought around baskets of supplies for the class project. "Choose your molds," she said at each table. "We're going to use a very simple method to make chocolates."

Molly and the others sorted through the molds, which featured hearts and flowers. They each selected a tray that would make twelve to fifteen candies.

Devon had them whip up a filling for the chocolates, choosing from several flavors—strawberry, vanilla, apricot, and coconut. While that cooled, they tempered chocolate, then "painted" the molds with a layer of it.

"Next you're going to inject the filling into each shell," Devon instructed.

The students readied their pastry bags and tips, a step the Bakehouse Three were quite familiar with. First, they squeezed filling into the molds, trying to be as uniform as possible, then sealed in the filling with another layer of chocolate. When the candy set and was removed from the molds, they could personalize the bonbons with sprinkles, shavings of chocolate, or piped swirls.

"I'm going to label these as mine," Carol said, piping a dark chocolate *C* on each milk chocolate candy. "I think I'll intertwine H and C when we do the next batch."

"That's a cute idea," Molly said. She'd chosen to sprinkle her coconut candies with shreds of white chocolate and coconut as if they'd been snowed upon.

Bridget had topped each chocolate with a red candy heart, and Laura had created a delicate design with piping and shavings.

Devon strolled around the room, checking each student's progress. From where she stood, Molly saw a lot of individuality on display. She mulled over options for designs she thought Fergus might appreciate. Maybe she could use a mold with a thistle, the flower of Scotland.

"You're all doing such a nice job," Devon said as he returned to the front. "Lots of natural talent in this room."

The students exclaimed with pleasure as they examined each other's chocolates.

"In fact." Devon raised a finger, waiting until the group quieted down. "We've randomly chosen several of your pieces for taste tests. My goal—besides indulging in some delicious chocolate—is to provide feedback." He shifted toward Robina, who was hovering on the sidelines. "Who are our three lucky winners?"

She came forward and, with dramatic intensity, read off three names. The last was Carol MacCallan.

All eyes on her, Carol gasped and smiled. Then her face grew comically fearful. "What if you don't like my chocolates?"

"I'm not worried," Devon said with a laugh. "You used my recipe to make the filling, so if you're good at following directions, it should be fine."

Robina sent him an angry glare, but when the camera swung to face her, her expression was calm again. Had Molly imagined the flash of bitterness? She thought not, and with the comment she'd overheard earlier, it sounded as if there might be some contention between host and assistant.

"I'm very good at following instructions," Carol said. "Ask Laura. She's Bread on Arrival's head pastry chef."

Nice way to sneak in a mention of our business.

Even better, Devon picked up on it. "Folks, you really ought to stop by Bread on Arrival here in Loch Mallaig when you have a chance. They make the most scrumptious Scottish-themed baked goods around."

The camera swung to focus on the Bakehouse Three and Bridget, who smiled and waved, then it was back to Devon.

"I'll take four candies each from the selected students," Devon said. "Robina will come around and get them for me. Your family and friends can enjoy the rest."

And with that, class was over. Robina approached Carol and collected four of her *C*-marked chocolates, then went around to the others. Molly packed her candy in a little plastic bag provided to them. "At least we have snacks for the faire," she said with a grin.

Carol checked her phone. "Speaking of which, Harvey wants to know when we'll be there."

"Half an hour?" Molly suggested. They had to clean up their stations and drive over, plus she wanted to stop at home and put on warmer clothes. Glancing around for Robina, who was supposed to bring a cart by for dirty dishes, she spotted the assistant standing in the corner, whispering to Blane. Dr. Dunbar had been hovering near the shop owner, and now she strode across the room to the door and slipped out.

Molly wondered if the professor and Devon were still on the outs after their heated discussion at the bakehouse that morning. The discovery of Marla's body seemed to be putting a wedge between friends, although in the case of Blane and Devon, the jealousies and disagreements were long-standing. Why was Blane attending the classes if he believed Devon had stolen his recipes? To cause trouble? Or seek proof?

Whatever his motivation, Molly sensed that more turmoil was on the horizon.

At home, Molly changed into clothing appropriate for tromping around outdoors. This included fleece-lined leggings under her jeans and a thermal top worn beneath a flannel plaid shirt. Cushy insulated wool socks went on her feet.

"You're wondering what I'm up to, aren't you, Angus?" Molly smiled at her pet, who was sitting in the bedroom doorway. She wouldn't have been able to sneak out without his notice if she'd tried. "Well, guess what? You're coming with me tonight."

She firmly believed that Angus could understand her a lot of the time and his response to her words only confirmed that. He bounced and whined, excited to take a walk. Darkness and cold temperatures couldn't deter Angus from the great outdoors.

"If you weren't a dog, you'd be a mail carrier," she told him, thinking of the famous motto about the challenges faced by intrepid delivery personnel.

Once Molly was dressed, she brushed her hair and put on fresh lipstick. Leaning closer to the mirror, she studied her face. Falling in love did wonders for a woman's complexion, and her eyes hadn't been this bright and sparkling in years.

She decided against a handbag tonight, wanting to stay light and unencumbered, so she zipped a small wallet into one coat pocket and her phone into another. Angus had eaten his dinner, but she brought along a few dog biscuits for later, tucking them into yet another pocket along with the bag of chocolates she'd made.

Her heart leaped when someone knocked on the door. Angus gave a tiny yip, then sat with his tail sweeping the floor behind him, knowing who was on the other side.

"Good evening." Fergus walked in, bringing cold fresh air and a hint of aftershave with him. He took off his hat, revealing ruffled dark locks threaded with gray. "Almost ready?"

Molly wanted to reach up and smooth his hair into place but she refrained. "I need to put on my outdoor clothes and leash Angus."

"I can take care of Angus." He grabbed the leash off the coat peg, and Angus sprinted toward him.

She slipped into her coat and boots, then pulled on a hat and gloves. "Ready."

Fergus, still holding the leash, opened the outside door for Molly to precede him. He was always scrupulously polite, a habit that made Molly feel cherished.

They went down the stairs, Angus thumping down step by step, then out the gate and to the sidewalk. When there wasn't snow and ice, Molly sometimes cut through her backyard into the adjacent park. Tonight they would go around on the street to Dumfries Park's main entrance.

Lively music drifted their way as they trudged along the sidewalk, fresh snow squeaking under their boots. The air was still but frosty, tingling in Molly's nose and lungs. She walked along at a good clip, knowing that was how she would stay warm.

Fergus tilted his head and studied the starlit sky. "What a beautiful night."

"It is." Molly moved a little closer to him. "But if the faire wasn't happening, I'd be very happy to stay inside."

He smiled down at her. "Me too. But I always feel so virtuous after braving inclement weather. Don't you?"

"It makes us Yoopers tough," Molly said with a laugh. If there was anything that united local residents, it was the weather. Hot, cold, stormy, calm—it was always worthy of note.

"You've got that right," Fergus said with a chuckle. "How was your class tonight?"

Molly told him how they'd made chocolates in a mold. "Want to try a piece?" She stopped and pulled out the bag. "Oops, those are Angus's treats." She put that bag back and grabbed the other. "Here we go."

She let him select his own, watching carefully while he popped it into his mouth and chewed. Angus whined, so she gave him a treat as well.

"Yum," Fergus finally said. "Very tasty." Angus crunched away, his version of voicing approval.

"You're not just saying that, are you?" Molly asked anxiously as they started walking again. She hadn't tried one yet, and she felt a sudden worry that they were terrible.

"Not at all." That heartwarming grin again. "You ought to have one yourself before I eat them all."

"Oh you." Molly selected her own chocolate and took a bite. The confection melted in her mouth with an explosion of dark chocolate and coconut. "It is good. Devon certainly gave us quality ingredients to work with. And guess what?" She told him how Devon was going to critique Carol's candy. "She was pretty excited to get feedback from the master himself."

"That's great," Fergus said. "I'm sure Harvey will appreciate her efforts too."

"No doubt of that. We'll all be making chocolate for the special people in our lives." She nudged him. "Including you."

"Lucky me." Fergus tucked Molly's hand in his elbow. "Are we all set for the Valentine's Day dance?"

Molly's heart lifted. "Are you asking me to go with you?" He hadn't officially invited her but they had discussed attending the event with the rest of the gang.

Fergus pulled her closer. "Who else would I go with? You're my best girl."

How sweet that sounded. "I'll need to buy a new dress." Molly might be able to dig something out of her closet but she wanted something perfect, to celebrate being with Fergus.

"Whatever you wear, you'll be beautiful," Fergus said gallantly.

They had reached the park. Normally at this time of year, the snowy expanse would be lit only with occasional streetlamps along the paths. Tonight, however, the area held cheerfully lit booths and trailers offering goods, games, and food, a stage where a Scottish duo played folk songs, and a section devoted to snow and ice sculptures.

A hand shot up from a small group near the entrance. Recognizing Carol, Molly said, "There they are," and steered Fergus and Angus in the direction of their friends.

Carol and Harvey stood with Laura and Trent. Tall, with dark hair and green eyes, Trent loved the outdoors as much as Laura, and the pair enjoyed many adventures together. To Molly's surprise, Bridget and Fergus's son, Neil, were also part of the group.

"Hi, Molly," Bridget said. "Neil and I were supposed to meet up with some other friends, but they didn't show."

"We're tagging along with you, if that's okay," Neil added.

"No problem," Molly said, noticing how attractive Bridget and Neil looked together. They were good friends, she knew, but based on the way Neil was gazing at Bridget, was it possible that something more was brewing?

Molly put her speculations aside. If something was beginning between Bridget and Neil, they would all find out about it in time.

Harvey, wearing the plaid tam complete with pompom Carol had bought him in Scotland, popped a chocolate into his mouth. "Carol's chocolates are so good. Want one?" He held the bag out to Fergus and Molly.

"Sure," Fergus said, selecting one and taking a bite. "Oh, nice. Apricot."

Molly had one too, and then Angus required another treat of his own. "These are delicious, Carol. You've got the touch."

Carol beamed. "I hope Devon likes them."

While the group walked toward the faire booths, Fergus asked Harvey, "How's the new chain saw? I heard it's been getting some use."

Harvey gladly gave the details, including make, model, and cutting ability.

"Harvey and his new toy," Carol said fondly.

They found the smoked sausage booth, an indulgence Molly justified by the rich meat's fuel-providing power for a cold night. Fergus bought her a so-called small portion—a six-inch toasted and buttered bun crammed with peppers, onions, and locally made sausage.

"My mouth is watering," Molly said as she dispensed mustard onto her sandwich.

"Mine too," Laura said, taking a big bite of her own.

Angus was going nuts over the smell of roasting meat, so Molly let him have a morsel of sausage. The group stood and ate, then bought tall cups of hot chocolate from another booth that they sipped as they wandered through the faire.

"Did Alastair catch up with you?" Molly asked Fergus while they were listening to the singing duo.

"About The Piping Yoopers playing for The Leaping Lowlanders performance?" Fergus asked. "He sure did. I can't wait to see you dancing on ice, Bridget."

"It's going to be fun," Bridget said, giving a little twirl. She frequently performed solos in the dance troupe. "At first I wasn't too sure about it, but Dallis has a friend with an indoor ice rink so we've been practicing a lot. Hopefully we'll surprise everyone with our grace and skill."

"I'll be there," Neil said. "Next stop, the Ice Capades?"

"I don't think so," Bridget said, her cheeks taking on a rosy hue that Molly didn't think had anything to do with the weather. "I'm just hoping to stay out of the hospital."

Molly smiled at their banter, then fell in step with Fergus. "This faire is a wonderful event," she said. "People are out here mingling with their neighbors instead of hibernating at home."

"I think that's the whole idea," Fergus said. "Plus, it gives us local businesses a boost."

"Devon Macintosh mentioned that he's staying at the resort," Molly said. "Have you met him?"

"Not officially," Fergus said. "But I did see him after your class when I came to get you."

"Oh, right." That whole evening was a blur in her mind. First the power outage, then the scare of the tree falling—and the even greater shock of discovering Marla's skeleton.

"So far he's a pretty low-key guest," Fergus said. "No demands on the staff. Stays in his suite a lot of the time."

"I probably would too, if I were a television star," Molly said. "The attention must be tiring. He did come to the bakehouse this morning with Dr. Dunbar from Superior Bay. They knew each other in college, I understand." Had it really been this morning? It felt like years ago.

She forced herself away from thoughts of Devon and his group of friends, instead making herself pay attention to the present moment.

The frosty air. The lilting music. The company of her best friends, including her loyal Angus.

"Want to check out the ice sculptures?" Laura asked. "They're not finished yet, but I'd like to see how far they got today."

"The theme is fairy tales, so they should be a lot of fun," Carol said.

The sculptures were located in a playing field, a sizable and level spot for the sprawling creations. As they drew closer, Molly saw shapes looming up from the snow and was instantly impressed at their large scale. Only a few lights illuminated the area, including spotlights aimed at the works of icy art.

"Oh, it's Rapunzel's tower," Bridget said eagerly. The structure was about twenty feet high, complete with carved steps circling up inside. "I'd love to go up."

"Not yet," Neil said, pointing out the rope barring the way, along with a sign that said, *Keep out—for now.*

Molly gazed up at the tower, noting the battlements around the edge on top that likely offered a good view of the faire. Maybe tomorrow they could go up.

The group moved on to the next sculpture, a miniature version of Cinderella's castle. This time, sawhorses barred the way into a couple of rooms.

"They must have to make sure the snow is really solid," Fergus commented. "Wouldn't want those ceilings to collapse on someone's head."

Molly shivered at the idea. "That would be scary."

As they circled the castle toward the next sculpture—the thatched cottage Snow White had shared with the seven dwarves—Angus whined and pulled on the end of his leash.

"Hush, boy," Molly said, pulling the leash gently. "What's wrong?" Perhaps her dog's sensitive nose had discerned the presence of other people ahead. She didn't see anyone moving around or hear voices, though.

Instead of settling down, Angus tugged even harder, forcing Molly to run forward. "Angus. Stop." Laughing, she glanced back over her shoulder at her friends. "I don't know what's gotten into him."

Then she understood. Angus stopped and whined, putting his paws up on a flat platform in front of the cottage.

A man was resting on the platform, hands folded on his chest. Molly's first thought was that he was sleeping, although that would be a dangerous move in these temperatures. But as she drew closer, she realized the truth.

A lifeless Devon Macintosh lay on what was meant to be Snow White's bier, clasping a small chocolate in his hands.

It was decorated with a swirling *C*, identical to the ones Carol had so carefully piped on her chocolates.

7

Molly rushed forward, intent on trying to help Devon. She pulled off a glove and tried to find a pulse in his neck. Nothing. Then she put a hand in front of his face to discern if he was exhaling warm air. Again, nothing.

She inhaled a deep, shuddering breath as she stepped backward, not wanting to contaminate the scene. Fortunately Angus had settled down, as if he realized that Devon was beyond any help she could give.

Footsteps crunched on the snow, and Fergus called, "Molly? Where are you?"

"Over here," Molly answered, her tone urgent. "Come quick. We have an emergency."

His footsteps sped up, followed by others as their friends caught on. Once he appeared on the scene, Fergus took in the situation at once. "Is he—"

Molly nodded, the thickening in her throat not allowing her to speak. She could scarcely take in the fact that Devon Macintosh, so vibrant earlier this evening, was dead.

"Call the police," she finally croaked. "I already checked for a pulse. There isn't one."

Ever efficient, Fergus strode off a step or two and dialed, the screen of his phone reflecting light on his chiseled features.

Everyone else arrived, taking in the scene with cries of horror and alarm. "This is tragic," Trent said, eyes wide with shock. "He looks so young."

"He is," Molly said. She did the math in her head, adding eleven years—the date of Marla's disappearance—to the usual college graduate age. "Early thirties, I think."

Carol let out a muted shriek. "Why does Devon have one of my chocolates in his hands?"

"That's yours?" Harvey asked. "Ah, it's got your trademark design. Oh, honey." He held out his arms to Carol, who curled into his embrace.

Why would Devon be holding one of Carol's candies, of all things? Had someone placed it there on purpose? Or had he been eating them when—

"It almost feels staged," Molly said, preferring this theory to the coincidence she'd been considering.

Laura frowned. "It sure does. He's lying on that slab like Snow White after she ate the apple." She surveyed the cottage. "Clearly the theme of this sculpture."

Bridget put a hand on Molly's arm. "Could they have chosen this place on purpose? I suppose there's a slim chance he might have lain down to rest, but why here, outside?"

"It's way too cold to take a nap out here," Neil said. "But if he did, not realizing that, he might have succumbed to hypothermia." Hypothermia was far from unknown in the Upper Peninsula, especially in the winter.

"He could have died of natural causes," Trent suggested. "I've seen a few young guys succumb to heart attacks."

And lie down peacefully with hands clasped? Molly doubted that.

"With no visible injuries, the coroner will have to determine cause of death," Fergus said as he put away his phone. "The police are on their way."

The group of friends huddled to one side while they waited for the authorities to arrive. Molly shivered as the minutes ticked by. Maybe it was her imagination, or the fact that she was standing still, but the temperatures seemed to be dropping fast. A frigid little breeze blew off the loch, sneaking down collars and up under hats.

"Are you doing okay?" Fergus asked Molly. They were standing shoulder to shoulder, and Angus was draped over the top of Molly's boots. He didn't like hanging around outside on nights like this either.

"I guess." Molly shrugged. Echoing the environment outside was the cold shock at her core. Devon Macintosh was gone. And it was very possible that he had been murdered. The question that naturally followed was this: Was his death related to the discovery of Marla Bannerman's skeleton?

Lights flashed as police cars entered the park, followed by an ambulance. At Fergus's direction, they'd taken a service road rather than approach through the main event area. Molly was sure that even with this precaution, word would soon get out and people would flock in this direction, curious to find out why the authorities were here.

"Who's in charge of the faire?" she asked Fergus. "Mayor Calhoun?"

He caught on right away. "You're right. He needs to be informed." Fergus scrolled through his phone contacts and found the mayor's number. "They'll definitely want to cordon off this area of the faire tonight, possibly longer." Again, he politely stepped away to place the call.

Two police cruisers and the ambulance ground to a halt in a parking area a short distance away.

Trent tugged his hat more snugly over his ears. "Do you want me to go meet them and guide them over here?"

"Good idea," Molly agreed. As the primary witness, she wasn't going to budge an inch until dismissed. And since either Devon or the killer had chosen to involve Carol's chocolates, her friend was also a lead witness. Horror flashed over Molly as realization hit. *Or a suspect.*

Molly was trying to ignore the churning unease in her midsection caused by this disconcerting idea when Chief Thomson and several officers arrived. The chief regarded the group. "Where is he?"

"Right over here, Chief," Fergus said, leading the investigators over to the site. "Molly discovered him. I made the call."

Molly flinched a little when Chief Thomson raised an eyebrow at her. "I'll need a statement, Molly. And team, let's get some lights out here."

"We'd better secure the area," Officer Anderson said. "We're going to have quite an audience any minute."

The chief glanced toward the faire, where throngs of people still milled about. "You're right about that. I'm surprised they're not already here." He snorted. "Along with the press."

The press. Devon Macintosh's death would be national news. Loch Mallaig had better brace itself for an influx of reporters and film crews.

"Mayor Calhoun is on his way," Fergus said. "He can direct your officers on the best way to seal off this section of the park."

"Thank you, Fergus," Chief Thomson said. "Now if you can all wait over there, someone will take your statements soon. It's a cold night to be standing around." He directed them to another spot in the field, well out of the way.

While they watched, the crime scene team put up spotlights and got to work, people going back and forth between the area and the emergency vehicles. Chief Thomson was conferring with local coroner and funeral home director Oliver Fitzgerald when Officer Anderson came over to Molly's group.

"All right, folks," Greer said. "I'm going to take your statements and let you get out of here. Who was first on the scene?"

"That was me," Molly said. "With Angus." She gave his leash to Fergus to hold.

Greer tilted her head to indicate Molly should step away from her friends. Once they were out of earshot, the officer said, "All right. Take it from the top."

From past experience, Molly knew that she should provide the full story—why and when she'd arrived at the park, the people she was with and their movements, and how Angus had alerted her to Devon's presence.

"Did you touch the deceased?" Officer Anderson asked.

"Yes," Molly admitted. "I checked for a pulse on his neck. I also held my hand in front of his nose and mouth to see if he was breathing, but that's all. Fergus showed up right after and he called 911."

"You recognized the deceased?" It wasn't really a question since Greer had seen Molly at the chocolate class after the tree came down, but the officer was using a voice recorder, so she needed to be thorough.

"Right away," Molly said with a shiver. "It's Devon Macintosh. I've been attending his chocolate-making classes at Superior Bay College. I went to one tonight before coming over here." She wondered if she should say something about the chocolate Devon was clutching, then decided that was Carol's information to share. Right now, there was no indication that the candy was a contributing factor in Devon's demise.

"How did he seem to you at the class tonight?" Greer asked next.

Molly thought back. "He was fine. Entertaining and funny, but that's his job, right? I didn't notice anything unusual." She thought of Blane's accusations of recipe theft, of Robina's disgruntlement with her boss, and about Devon's sudden departure from the bakehouse while meeting with Dr. Dunbar—but she held all that back for now. Maybe Devon had died of natural causes, such as an unknown health problem. Until the cause of death was identified, all this was mere speculation.

"Is there something else you want to share, Mrs. Ferris?" As befitted the recording, Officer Anderson was all business. She also knew Molly well and could tell she was holding something back.

"Nothing related to tonight," Molly said. "But I have observed that Devon had some conflicts with those around him."

"Like what?"

"I'm afraid I don't have specific information. Well, except that Blane Tully of Tully's Treats thinks Devon stole some recipes back when he worked there as a teenager. His assistant, Robina, appears to resent him. And he and Dr. Dunbar had some kind of disagreement at the bakehouse this morning, though I didn't hear the conversation." Even to Molly's ears, she heard how lame this all sounded. Certainly nothing that pointed to a murder motive. Would someone kill over a stolen recipe? She thought it was a possibility if the thief had gone on to fame and fortune with it and the original owner was stuck in a shabby shop in a small town.

Apparently Officer Anderson didn't find much to probe in Molly's revelations because she didn't ask any further questions. "You can go now, Mrs. Ferris. Please send Mr. MacGregor over."

Molly rejoined the group and relayed the message to Fergus. "Do you want to wait for me, Molly?" he asked as he handed Angus's leash back to her. "If not, I understand. You must be freezing."

"I'm okay," she said. "I'll wait." After he trotted off, Molly went to Carol. "I didn't tell her that Devon is holding your chocolate. I figured that was up to you to share."

Carol set her chin. "And I plan to. What a terrible coincidence that it was my candy. He had other student chocolates to eat besides mine, plus all his own chocolates."

"I wonder if there's a message there," Bridget said. "I have no idea what the message could be, but I feel certain that it's significant."

Molly thought again that the whole thing had struck her as staged. If Devon was murdered, had the killer chosen Carol's chocolate on purpose? Her spirits sagged at the thought, and she prayed that her friend wouldn't be dragged into a murder investigation.

Fergus didn't spend long with Officer Anderson. "Who's next?" he asked when he rejoined the circle. "She said it was up to us to decide." The others in the group knew even less than Molly and Fergus since they'd been last on the scene.

Carol squared her shoulders. "I'll go. Wish me luck."

While Carol was interviewed, everyone else stood in silence. Molly noticed that people had drifted over from the faire, kept at bay by sawhorses and an officer barring the path. She could hear the babble of excited voices and questions from here. At the crime scene, mercifully out of public view, two EMTs were gently placing Devon on a gurney. The wheels caught on snow and ice as they rolled him away.

Fergus released a sighing breath. "That poor man. I hope they find answers soon."

"Me too," Molly said fervently.

Carol trudged back from her chat with Greer. "Who's next?"

"Harvey, why don't you go?" Laura suggested. "Then you and Carol can head home."

"Are you sure?" Harvey asked.

"We don't mind waiting," Trent confirmed.

"How'd it go?" Molly asked Carol as Harvey tramped off through the snow.

"Okay." Carol shrugged. "She didn't seem to think much about it being my candy. In fact, she asked me about the recipe."

Laura's eyes met Molly's, and Molly understood immediately. Was Officer Anderson's question casual interest or was there another motivation?

Molly shook her head, annoyed with herself. "I wouldn't mind getting going," she said to Fergus. "I'm exhausted. Do the rest of you mind if we leave?"

The others insisted that was fine, so Molly, Fergus, and Angus set off down the path. They could have exited the other way, but that would have meant going through where the authorities were set up, and Molly didn't think they'd appreciate that.

At the barrier, Molly recognized Officer Dalziel Murdoch, the youngest member of the force. He blinked at them, then cleared his throat. "You want to get by?"

"Please," Fergus said. "We just finished talking to the chief and Officer Anderson."

"Stand back," Officer Murdoch bellowed. "People coming through." He moved the sawhorse enough that Molly and Fergus could sidle by.

Having Angus trotting ahead of them helped clear the way, Molly noted. As they made their way through the throng, Molly heard snatches of sentences revealing that the identity of the victim was already out. It often amazed her how fast information spread. It had always been this way in small towns like this one, even before the Internet and worldwide connectivity.

A figure ran toward them, arms pumping. As the person drew closer, Molly recognized Dr. Dunbar. The professor halted abruptly when she spotted Molly and Fergus. "Is it true?" she asked urgently. "Is Devon dead?" She spoke loudly enough that bystanders nearby gaped at her.

Molly steeled herself. Sharing bad news was never easy. "I'm afraid so," she said in a gentle voice. "They don't know—"

"No! No, it can't be true." Dr. Dunbar darted around Molly and Fergus, barreling toward the flashing police lights, the watching crowd, and the policeman at the barrier.

"He won't let her through," Fergus murmured, watching over his shoulder.

They began walking again. "No," Molly said. "But I don't blame her for trying. She must be devastated." Had Devon's other friends and companions gotten wind yet? She swallowed as she realized there could be one among them who was glad the news was out—the person who killed him.

8

Molly was definitely bleary-eyed when she arrived in the bake-house kitchen the next morning. "Coffee," she rasped, glad to see Laura had already made a pot.

Laura glanced up from her work with a laugh. "That bad, huh? I can relate. Trent and I were up until after midnight." Her lips twisted in a rueful smile. "Mostly talking about Devon Macintosh. Both of us were in shock. Honestly, I think I still am."

"Me too." Molly chose the largest mug she could find and filled it almost to the brim, leaving barely enough room for cream. "As you can probably tell by the circles under my eyes, I had trouble falling asleep."

"And the bags under mine have grown from carry-on to full-size," Laura joked. "Are you going to be able to race today?"

"Oh no." Molly had forgotten about the snowshoe race later this morning. Her limbs felt like spaghetti. She gulped down a reviving mouthful of coffee. "Maybe I'll have more energy by then."

Laura was rolling out dough on the counter. "Try a red velvet scone when they're done and you'll be all set."

"You're making red velvet today? Yum." Molly enjoyed red velvet cake, so she was anxious to try Laura's new confection.

"With cream cheese drizzle," Laura said, wielding the heart-shaped cutter. "Can't have red velvet without cream cheese."

The back door opened and shut and Carol entered the kitchen. "Brr. It's a chilly one out there." She slipped off her outerwear and boots.

"Let me get you a coffee." Molly found another large mug, figuring Carol was tired too.

This theory was confirmed when Carol sighed deeply. "I barely got a wink all night," she said as she reached for an apron. "And when I did sleep, I had the worst dreams."

Laura frowned sympathetically. "Sounds like you need a red velvet scone too."

Carol's expression brightened. "I love red velvet." She took the mug of coffee from Molly with thanks, perching on a stool to drink. After a few hasty sips, she said, "I assume the class is canceled. Have either of you heard anything?"

"I can't imagine they'll go on with it," Molly said. "Especially since they were filming for Devon's show."

Laura arranged scones on a baking tray. "I've heard stranger things. Hate to say it, but the ratings would be through the roof, and that's how a lot of those decisions are made."

Carol's upper lip curled. "Talk about heartless."

Curious to see what the media was saying, Molly picked up her phone. "The news has gone national," she announced. "Not that I'm surprised."

"Do any of them mention the cause of death?" Carol asked.

Molly perused the articles. "No, not yet." A certain sentence caught her eye. "Oh, get this. Robina McDonald, Devon's assistant, says that they will continue filming in Loch Mallaig as a tribute to Devon, who went to school here."

"There's our answer," Laura said. She picked up the tray of scones and headed for the oven. "Set the timer, will you, Carol? You two can try a couple from this first batch."

While the scones baked, Molly and Carol bustled around getting the bakehouse ready to open. Laura started a batch of her melt-in-the-mouth shortbread, another customer favorite. Once the timer rang and the scones cooled and were frosted, they did the taste test.

"Scrumptious," Molly declared. "I love it."

"Me too." Carol nodded with enthusiasm. "They're going to sell out fast."

Laura grinned. "I'd better make some more then."

From the minute they opened, the bakehouse was busy. Bridget and Hamish arrived midmorning, which allowed Molly to go to her race.

"You're racing on snowshoes?" Hamish asked Molly as she took off her apron. "It's not exactly easy to run on those things, you know." He pretended to waddle back and forth along the kitchen floor. "They're made for wading in deep snow."

"I know," Molly said. "That's the challenge. But I'm fueled by coffee and scones."

"Like any good Scottish lass," Hamish said with approval as he picked up a tray of clean mugs and plates. "Good luck to you."

Good luck to me, indeed, Molly thought as she dashed upstairs to change. At least she'd get to see Fergus, since he'd promised to come watch. He could take her for hot chocolate afterward as a consolation prize.

Dressed in base layers, a fleece jacket, and top-and-bottom wind shells, Molly walked over to the park, clutching her snowshoes. The sculpture area was still off-limits, with yellow caution tape draped between sawhorses.

A cluster of people was gathered at the race check-in point, milling around as they waited for the race to begin. Molly's heart gave a jump when she saw Fergus's tall figure among them.

"I'm glad you made it," he said when she approached him. "After last night's ordeal, I was wondering if you'd have second thoughts."

"Me too," Molly said with a laugh. She scanned the crowd and spotted the sign-in desk. "Let me check in, then I'll be right back."

"I'll hold your snowshoes," he offered, and she handed them over.

At the desk, Molly gave her name, then received a paper bib that she pulled over her head and pinned to her jacket. "This is a timed race," the young woman behind the desk told her. "You'll go in waves, and winning times will be compiled after, by class." She squinted at Molly. "Under forty, right?"

Molly burst out laughing. "I wish. Try adding a decade, and then some." Her sunglasses must be doing a good job of hiding the laugh lines around her eyes.

"Really?" The young woman smiled in surprise. "You look great."

"Thank you," Molly said with sincerity as she pinned on her bib. "You just made my day."

Fergus, who had been lingering nearby, had overheard. "You are lovely," he said, giving her a quick kiss. "I like a woman dressed in sporting gear."

"Good thing," Molly said, taking back her snowshoes. "My designer wardrobe is pretty threadbare." Which reminded her that she needed to buy a new dress for Valentine's Day. She wanted something absolutely stunning.

After strapping on the snowshoes, Molly joined the racers near the starting line. At intervals, groups were released to run the course, which led through an open area and then veered into the woods. Molly was already familiar with the trail since she often walked it during better weather.

Molly's group was called next. She edged up to the starting line, glancing at her fellow competitors. As a young man bent his long legs, poised to dash, an older, heavyset woman gave Molly a complicit smile. "Slow and steady wins the race," she said.

A good reminder. Even with Molly's small, sleek snowshoes, she still had to stand in an almost bowlegged position. If she wasn't careful, she would tread on her own equipment and fall flat. How did she know? She'd done it before—more than once.

And they were off, Fergus yelling, "Go, Molly, go!" She plodded along, trying to concentrate on putting one foot in front of the other. The young man was already down, snow covering his clothing. As Molly went by, he picked himself up and swiped at the snow. The older woman was ahead, her wide body rocking back and forth as she wielded her snowshoes expertly.

The trail entered the woods, guiding Molly between rows of snow-frosted evergreens. The forest was quiet and hushed, with only a slight breeze in the treetops. Here and there, trails of tiny footprints crossed the snow, signs of animal life.

Everything felt different in the winter, as if made new. Molly wished she could stop and take pictures, but in the middle of a race, she'd settle for snapping mental photos. She should come out here again soon with Angus and Fergus.

The trail went out and around before circling back toward Crag Mallaig, a rock formation in the center of the park. This time of year, it was adorned with small icicles and capped with snow. Sun glinted through the trees, making the ice sparkle.

"Hurry up," a woman's voice said from around the corner. "I'm freezing."

Other racers up ahead? Keeping her pace steady, Molly skirted the crag.

"That's it. I'm done," a male voice said.

The woman laughed. "I'll decide that."

Molly smiled at the banter. Despite what the man said, it didn't make sense to quit now. It was equally as far back to the beginning as it was to continue. Maybe they didn't realize the racecourse was a big loop.

As Molly came around the outcropping, she saw a male figure wearing a hooded orange shell dashing off on another trail that led to the far side of the park. He really was serious about quitting.

Then she recognized the woman standing in the shelter of a large pine. "Dr. Dunbar," Molly said as she approached. "I didn't know you were racing."

"Oh, Molly. You startled me." Dr. Dunbar took a step backward, causing her to brush against overhanging evergreen branches. Snow immediately slid off onto her head. She shrieked. "That went down my neck."

"Don't you hate that?" Molly asked. She didn't stop. "Sorry. I'd love to chat, but I need to keep going." She kept trudging forward, not waiting to see if Dr. Dunbar was following. She had reached the halfway point, and new energy coursed through her muscles.

Molly crossed the finish line to cheers and the ringing of cowbells. But her gaze was fastened on the beaming man waiting to greet her.

"Way to finish strong," Fergus said. "I have some drinks for you once you catch your breath." He held a bottle of water and a cup of hot chocolate.

"Thanks so much." Molly accepted the water bottle and guzzled it down. "I wonder how I did."

"They said it takes a while to compile the times." Fergus took the empty water bottle and handed her the hot chocolate. "The food trucks and booths are open, so I thought we could get some lunch, then come back."

"I saw a ramen truck. How does that sound?" Molly asked, thinking a large serving of hot, savory broth and noodles sounded perfect right now.

"I was hoping you'd say that." Fergus waited while Molly took off her snowshoes, then they strolled to the vendor area. The park was already quite full of visitors. Children were sliding down a man-made hill, screeching with joy while their parents watched. Booths sold handmade crafts such as knitted and crocheted hats and scarves, hosted games, and promoted local businesses.

They found a sheltered place in the sun to enjoy their soup. Out on the loch, skaters circled. "The Lowlanders are rehearsing," Fergus observed.

Molly grimaced. "Thanks for reminding me. I haven't even looked at the set list yet."

"Nothing new. They're moving their regular numbers to ice, that's all."

"Good." Molly tipped her cup to get the last spoonful of broth. "I really need to practice, though."

"Why don't we practice together?" Fergus suggested.

Molly smiled at him. "That would be much more fun than doing it alone. Oh, except for Angus, who tries to bury his head in sofa cushions when I play."

Fergus threw back his head and laughed. "Surely it's not that bad."

"Some days it can be," Molly said, though she had to admit that those days were fewer and farther between now than they had been when she'd first learned the instrument.

A figure in orange caught her eye. He was trotting along the path beside the loch but paused to observe the Lowlanders perform a country dance on ice. Was that the rogue snowshoe racer? She tried to get a glimpse of his face, but the hood and hat plus sunglasses effectively disguised him.

As they walked back to the starting line, Molly told Fergus about her encounter with Dr. Dunbar and her friend in the woods. "I have no idea how I did," she commented as they joined the group waiting for results. Not that she really cared, but now the moment was upon her, her midsection tightened with nerves.

The race coordinator who had complimented Molly read off results, with another volunteer handing out prizes like T-shirts and gift certificates.

"The winner of the women over fifty category is . . ." She paused dramatically, as she had each time. "Molly Ferris!"

Molly gasped and grabbed Fergus's forearm. "I won."

Fergus smiled down at her. "Congratulations. Go get your prize."

"Here I am," Molly called, edging to the front of the crowd. "I'm Molly Ferris."

She stood next to the coordinator while someone took their picture, then received an envelope. Back with Fergus, she opened it and chuckled. "Guess what? I won a gift certificate to the King's Heid Pub."

"Good," Fergus said. "You can take me out." He pecked her on the lips. "Just kidding. Give it to Carol. Or Laura."

"Or both." She could offer it to the group when they went to the Valentine's Day dinner to take a little off everyone's bill.

Fergus pulled out his phone. "I hate to say this, but I'd better run. I have meetings this afternoon. What do you have going on?"

"I have chocolate class later, but I'll be home after that."

His brows shot up. "Chocolate class? I'd assumed that was done, given what happened to the instructor."

Molly pulled a face. "Apparently his assistant is taking over. They're going to make it into a tribute to Devon."

"Anything to keep those ratings up," Fergus said wryly. "Sorry. That sounded cynical."

"No, I think you're right. Anyway, it should be interesting." Molly was not only curious to see how Robina handled the situation, she also hoped to figure out something else—namely, whether one of Devon's inner circle was guilty of murder.

9

"I'm back," Molly announced as she entered the bakehouse kitchen, freshly showered and wearing her usual attire.

"How did it go?" Laura asked. The day was winding down, and she was unloading clean baking utensils and pans from the dishwasher. Carol was carrying dirty dishes into the kitchen. Bridget and Hamish were out front.

Molly couldn't hold back a grin. "I won." At their exclamation, she added, "My age group, that is."

"Still, that's super," Carol said, setting down the tub of dishes with a clatter. "What did you get for a prize?"

"You'll never believe it." Molly paused. "A gift certificate to the King's Heid Pub."

Carol laughed. "That's almost like getting a gift certificate to Bread on Arrival."

"It is a bonus to have an in with the owner," Molly said. "Anyway, I'm donating it to you two for the Valentine's Day dinner."

Laura waved her off. "You don't need to do that. Trent is paying for my ticket."

"And we bought ours already," Carol said, filling a tray with mugs and plates. "Why don't we give it to Grizela? She can do a drawing that night and give it to one of the couples who attend." Grizela Duff, librarian and head of the local historical society, had arranged the dinner dance.

"I like that," Molly said, picturing the excitement the drawing would create. It was fun to give unexpected gifts. She found her phone. "I'll text her right now."

"Speaking of the dance, have you two decided what you're wearing yet?" Carol asked.

Molly sent her text, then pocketed her phone. "I need to go shopping."

"Me too," Laura said. "Why don't we stop by Happily Ever After? They have some nice formal wear." Although the shop specialized in wedding dresses, they also offered clothing for semiformal and formal occasions.

"We should go soon," Molly said. "If I don't find anything, I'm going to have to go out of town." The lack of shopping options was one of the few drawbacks to living in Loch Mallaig. Since Molly wasn't a huge shopper, most of the time she didn't care.

Bridget came through the kitchen door. "And we're closed, ladies. The last group just left."

"I'll go cash out," Molly said. "Are you still going to the chocolate class tonight, Bridget?"

The college student nodded. "I wouldn't miss it. I'm curious to see how Robina is going to pull this off. From behind the camera to star in one day."

Was that a motive for murder? Although Molly was fairly unfamiliar with the inner workings of cable television, she guessed that good opportunities were few and far between.

"That is quite a leap," Laura said. "Devon left some pretty big shoes to step into. He was a gifted chocolatier, but more importantly for a TV show, he had tons of personality and charisma. People wanted to watch and learn from him."

"Even if he did steal recipes," Bridget said. "I was so disappointed to hear that."

"He *allegedly* stole them," Carol reminded her. "You never know, Blane might have an ax to grind. It must rankle that his old friend went on to become famous."

"While he was left behind here in small-town Michigan," Molly added. Another person with a motive for murder. Sighing, she went to the door. "I'd better go take care of the register so we won't be late."

A short while later, Molly drove out to Superior Bay College, trailing behind the others. They'd normally carpool, but with Laura and Carol living on that side of town, it didn't make sense for them to double back to the bakehouse.

The sun was already sinking, although the days were much longer than they'd been a month ago. Molly cherished every extra minute, a sign that spring was right around the corner. At the college, she parked next to Carol's Chrysler. The other three were waiting for her, and they walked together toward the building.

A cluster of men and women stood outside the entrance. At first Molly thought they were lingering students, but their shouted words soon put an end to that.

"Are you here for *Chocolates by the Bay*?"

"Did you know Devon Macintosh?"

"How was he the last night of class?"

Molly cringed, glad that the reporters didn't know she'd found Devon. Fortunately, the newspapers had omitted that detail, saying only that a Winter Faire attendee had stumbled upon his body. She'd have to thank Chief Thomson when she saw him next.

The four women ducked their heads and pushed through to the door, where a college security guard was stationed. "Here for the class?" he asked. "Show me your identification."

Glad she didn't have to say her name out loud for the reporters to hear, Molly handed him her license, and he checked it against a list. After he cleared all of them, he opened the door so they could enter.

"This is crazy," Bridget whispered once they were in the hall. "I don't think I'd like being famous."

"Me neither," Molly said. "I like being a nobody." She smiled at the others. "Let me correct that. A nobody with the best friends ever."

"And dog," Carol said.

"Don't forget Fergus," Laura added. "Best man around. Besides Trent, Harvey, and Neil, I mean."

The women laughed. "We are fortunate," Carol said. "Keepers, all." Her gaze fell on Bridget. "Probably jumping the gun with you and Neil, though, Bridget."

"Definitely." Bridget's tone was airy. "Neil is a great friend."

Molly noticed Bridget was blushing again but kept quiet. If there was something between Neil and Bridget, it would blossom in due time.

Pandemonium greeted them in the classroom. Judging by the activity, Molly guessed that all the students had returned, and they had plenty to say. If anything, the press presence outside had raised the excitement level.

Seemingly unperturbed, Cole was busy setting up the camera and sound equipment.

The newcomers lined up at the sink behind a few other students to wash their hands before class. Assessing the line, Molly said, "I'll pop down to the restroom and use that sink."

The others opted to stay in the classroom, so Molly went down the hall alone. When she pushed through the door, she found Robina standing at a sink applying makeup.

"Hi, Robina," Molly said. "Getting ready?"

"Trying to." Devon's assistant gave a nervous laugh. Her fingers shook and she dropped the top of a lipstick into the sink, where it clattered. "I used to do Devon's makeup, so there's no one to help me." She leaned forward and applied the lipstick with more care than Molly had seen anyone use for that task. After finishing, she smacked her lips together. "Hopefully that will change when we go back to San Francisco."

Molly was struck by the implications of Robina's statement. "Are you taking over his shop?"

Robina lifted one shoulder in a shrug. "We'll see. But I'm definitely hoping to take over his cable slot." Catching Molly's eyes in the mirror, she said, "Does that sound heartless? The fact is, such opportunities are few and far between in this business."

"I'm sure," Molly said, trying to sound neutral despite the fact that Robina's bald ambition sounded like a possible motive for murder.

Robina dug through her makeup bag. "Besides, it's only fair."

Before Molly could ask what she meant by that, the door swung open again, revealing Dr. Dunbar. Seeing Robina, her brow creased in a ferocious scowl. Deciding to get out of the way, Molly ducked into a stall.

"How could you?" Dr. Dunbar growled at Robina. "Talk about dancing on Devon's grave."

After a brief pause, Robina said, "What else am I supposed to do? The network ordered the episodes, so I'm going to deliver. Besides, they'll be ratings gold."

Molly couldn't argue with that. People who had never watched Devon's show would be tuning in out of sheer curiosity.

"I'm trying to keep his legacy alive," Robina added. "I'd think, as his friend, that you'd want that too."

A tense silence fell. Molly could almost hear Dr. Dunbar's brain whirring as she sought the perfect answer.

"If you say so," the professor finally huffed. "It just seems awfully *convenient* to me."

Robina barked a laugh. "You think I had something to do with Devon dying? Why would I kill the golden goose, so to speak? Devon was planning to let me cohost a few episodes later this spring."

Was that true? If Robina's goal was to step in front of the camera, then that approach was a good way to learn the ropes and get comfortable.

Now the young woman had been flung into the deep end. No wonder her hands were shaking.

Dr. Dunbar made a scoffing sound, but she didn't pursue the topic any further. "Are you almost ready? Cole sent me to find you."

The two women exited the restroom, leaving Molly alone with her suspicions.

On the way back into the classroom, Molly narrowly avoided colliding with Cole as he stepped back from a camera. "Sorry," he said with a smile. "I didn't see you there."

"I wasn't here a moment ago," Molly said, laughing. "I'm hurrying to my seat."

"Don't worry, you have a few." Cole nodded toward the front of the room, where Dr. Dunbar and Robina were setting up the workstation. "They're still getting ready."

The students had settled down, Molly noticed, but were still chatting. She decided to take the opportunity to talk to Cole. "I'm so sorry for your loss. You worked closely with Devon, I take it?"

He nodded forlornly. "Yeah, for a few years now. I'll miss him."

"I'm sure." Molly remembered that she hadn't talked to Cole about Marla, another major loss in his life. "I was also sorry to hear about Marla. I know she meant a lot to you." His eyes flared in surprise and she hastily added, "Dr. Pryde told me that you two used to date."

"Dr. Pryde, huh?" His lips twisted in a sardonic smile. "Is he seriously still teaching? He was ancient when we had him. Or at least, that's how he is in my memory."

"When you're that young, everyone comes off as old," Molly said. And the reverse was true now. College students resembled children to her. "Yes, Dr. Pryde is still going strong. Bridget has him this year for Senior English."

Cole rolled his eyes. "Everyone's Waterloo, for sure. He was so tough. Even the smartest kids were afraid of failing."

"He still is," Molly said. He'd avoided saying anything about Marla, she noticed, and she wondered if she should press the issue. She opted for a more indirect approach. "He was pretty sad about Marla and said she was one of his best students."

"Yeah, she was brilliant," Cole confirmed. His expression grew nostalgic. "A little flaky, but fun. She often planned dorm-wide parties and tournaments. I was the reigning table tennis champ."

"I'll bet," Molly said. "It must have been such a shock when she disappeared."

A shadow fell across his face. "Yeah." He visibly swallowed. "I—we all thought she'd either drowned or killed herself. I kept going over everything in my mind, wondering if I could have prevented it from happening." He studied the floor, and his lips trembled. "I was pretty serious about that girl. I thought we had a future, even if it was rocky between us sometimes."

Molly remembered what Dr. Dunbar had said, that Marla was afraid of someone. Had it been Cole? Maybe, as Blane had claimed, she'd tried to break up with Cole so she could date Devon. And Cole had responded with anger.

More questions hovered on Molly's lips, but now was not the time to ask them. Robina was staring at Cole, obviously wanting to get his attention. "I think class is about to start," Molly said. "Talk to you later."

Cole muttered a reply and fiddled with the camera settings. Molly scooted to her station.

"What were you talking to Cole about?" Carol asked. The other two leaned close to listen to Molly's answer.

"I'll tell you later," Molly said, aware that the class was falling silent. "I also ran into Robina in the restroom. That was interesting as well."

"Can we talk at break?" Bridget whispered, her eyes pleading. "I'm dying to hear."

Molly nodded and faced forward again in time to catch Cole signal to Robina that he was rolling.

"Welcome, everyone, to this edition of Chocolates by the Bay," Robina said, then the smile dropped from her face. "As you all know, our show family experienced a tragedy this week."

Blane, who was slipping into the room, gave a nearly inaudible snort. Robina glared in his direction, then caught herself.

"Before we dive in, I'd like to have a moment of silence for Devon," Robina continued. The room was quiet for several seconds, many folks bowing their heads. Finally, Robina glanced at Dr. Dunbar, who held a small remote for the room's projector. "We've put together a montage to celebrate his life."

Music played as a series of scenes from Devon's life were projected onto a screen at the front of the room. Photos showed him in his shop, on a television show, . . . and at college. Molly had to bite back a gasp. The nudge in her ribs told her that Carol saw it too. A small group of friends—Devon, Dr. Dunbar, Blane, Cole, and Marla—hammed it up under the very tree that had fallen in the storm. With blonde hair flowing and a mischievous grin on her pretty features, Marla stood in the middle. She'd obviously been the center of this little band. And someone had resented her for it.

"That was so nice, wasn't it?" Robina said after the montage ended. She blinked a few times, hinting that she'd teared up, before setting her shoulders and shifting gears. "Today we're going to upgrade your skills. No more amateur hour. You're going to learn how to hand dip chocolates."

The students applauded, earning a grin from the new host.

"Remember the fillings you made yesterday?" Robina asked.

"You're going to use the rest of that today. Brianne is going to pass around your fillings, which need to come up to room temperature."

Clearly displeased at being addressed so informally, Dr. Dunbar pushed a cart of plastic tubs around the room. Each had been labeled with the student's name.

Dr. Dunbar arrived at Molly's table. "What are your names again?" she asked, having apparently forgotten them. After Molly gave hers, the professor handed her a container, a process that repeated with Laura and Bridget. When Carol spoke up, however, Dr. Dunbar shook her head. "I don't see it."

"How can that be?" Carol asked. She examined the remaining containers, peering at each name. "This is weird. I don't see it anywhere."

The professor bit her lip. "I don't know what to tell you." She peeked over her shoulder at the waiting students. "I need to hand out the rest of these."

"We'll share," Laura said to Carol. "Each of us can give you some. That way you'll have your own sampler platter."

"That will work," Molly said. "I have tons."

Carol still seemed troubled, but she accepted their offer, and they all scooped dollops of their fillings into clean bowls for her.

"All right, class." Robina clapped her hands sharply. "Chop your chocolate."

They went through the now-familiar steps of tempering chocolate, then began the dipping process. This involved using a long fork to hold the filling, which was swirled through the melted chocolate. More than one student lost a chunk of filling in the bowl and had to fish it out, prompting lots of laughter. Another trick was getting rid of excess chocolate before lifting the piece out of the bowl.

"I think I'm getting it," Bridget crowed. "Check this out." She pointed to the parchment paper, where her freshly made candy was resting.

"You're a natural," Laura said.

Bridget beamed at this praise from one of her mentors.

Someone rapped at the classroom door, and Molly saw Officer Greer Anderson peeking through the glass. What was she doing here?

Robina jerked her head up with a glare. She gestured for Cole to shut off the camera before stalking over to the door and opening it a crack. "Yes?" she asked testily.

The students fell silent to listen.

Officer Anderson spoke in a voice too low for them to hear, but a moment later, Robina opened the door wide to allow the officer and a couple of others to enter.

"I'm sorry to interrupt your hard work, but I've got a search warrant for this room," Greer announced. "Unfortunately, that means class is now over." Her serious gaze shifted to Carol. "And please stay, Mrs. MacCallan. We need to speak to you."

10

"Me?" Carol's face flushed as everyone in the room stared at her. "Why on earth do you want to speak to me?"

Officer Anderson didn't answer. Instead, she began to issue orders to her fellow officers.

Molly had an idea where this was heading, and she didn't like it one bit. "Hang in there, Carol," she whispered. "We'll figure it out."

The classroom had burst into noisy chatter as the students prepared to leave. Robina stood with the officers, her arms crossed. One officer was talking to Cole, who shook his head. Molly assumed they were asking for the video files.

Dr. Dunbar, who had been lurking in the rear, made her way to the front. She joined Robina and Officer Anderson, and when all three peered over at Carol, Molly guessed why with a sinking feeling. The missing filling was significant for some reason, as was the fact that Devon had been holding Carol's chocolate when he died. *Or someone placed it in his hands.*

An officer spoke to each student as they prepared to leave, taking down contact information. One by one they filtered out until Molly and her friends were the only students left. Robina, Dr. Dunbar, and Cole were still standing in a cluster, watching.

Officer Anderson came over to Molly's table. "You three have to leave," Greer said to Molly, Bridget, and Laura. "We need to talk to Carol by herself."

"Does she need an attorney?" Molly dug out her phone. "Carol, I think you'd better have one." Because of previous cases, Molly had the number of defense attorney Donal "Bulldog" McNab in her contacts.

Carol's brown eyes widened with alarm. "Really? Am I under arrest?"

Officer Anderson sighed. "No. We merely want to talk to you, Mrs. MacCallan."

"Because of my chocolates, right?" Carol asked. "Well, I can assure you that I had nothing to do with Devon's death." She forced a chuckle. "My candy might not be the greatest, but it won't kill you."

Bridget, who had been scrolling on her phone, gasped. "They do think it was the candy. Devon was poisoned."

Officer Anderson put a hand to her face with a groan. "How did they get the story already?" she muttered, more to herself than Molly and her friends.

Carol lifted her chin. "My chocolates were not poisonous. What a ridiculous idea. Harvey ate a bunch, and he's still walking around."

"I had one too, and I didn't even feel sick after," Laura said. "Greer, you've known Carol for years. She's not a killer. Besides, why would she poison Devon Macintosh? She didn't even know him."

The officer looked miserable. "I'm sorry, ladies. But I have to do my job." She glanced toward the front of the room, where Officer Michael Drummond was ushering Robina, Cole, and Dr. Dunbar out. "My team needs to get to work, so let's wrap this up."

"If Donal McNab can meet me at the station, I'll let you interview me, Officer Anderson." Carol drew herself up, a fierce expression on her face. "Otherwise, arrest me. Then I definitely won't talk until I have an attorney."

Officer Anderson was silent for a moment. "Give him a call, Molly. Now go on, get out of here. We need to search this room."

The Bakehouse Three and Bridget hastily gathered their things and moved out to the hallway.

"I can't believe this is happening," Carol said. "What a nightmare."

Laura and Bridget put their arms around her, murmuring soothing words.

Meanwhile, Molly was already pressing the dial button, hoping the attorney would answer. At this time of night, he was probably relaxing at home. To her relief, he picked up. "Hi, Mr. McNab. This is Molly Ferris calling." She proceeded to give him the facts, and he immediately offered to meet Carol at the station.

"Well?" Laura asked when Molly disconnected the call.

"He's on board," Molly told the others. "Leaving his house now."

Carol's hands shook as she pulled out her own phone. "I need to call Harvey and tell him what's going on."

"Laura, want to drive Carol to the station?" Molly suggested, seeing her friend's nervous state. "We can leave Carol's car here for the night, right, Bridget?"

"It should be fine," Bridget said. "I'll go over to the parking office and get an overnight pass. Don't leave without me."

Carol was talking to Harvey, tears spilling down her cheeks. "Okay, I'll wait for you before I go in. We're heading out in a few. Love you." After hanging up, she took the tissue Molly offered and wiped her eyes. "He's such a good man."

"He really is," Molly agreed. She was grateful that Carol had Harvey's support and love to carry her through this difficult situation. "We're going to get to the bottom of this, Carol. You know that, right?"

"Absolutely we are," Laura said. "We're going to find Devon's killer. It's beyond rotten that they tried to pin their crime on you."

Carol's tears flowed afresh. "I'm so glad to have you two in my corner." Her lips trembled. "This is really scary."

"Don't worry," Molly said. "Donal is on the case. He's one of the best defense attorneys in the state."

Carol smiled through her tears. "Thanks for reminding me. He's something else, isn't he?"

The exit door at the far end opened. "I have the parking pass," Bridget said, waving the hangtag. "But don't go out the regular door. The press is still here."

Hot on the scent of a new story, no doubt, with the police arriving tonight. "Lead on, Bridget," Molly said. "Carol, give me your keys. I'll put the pass in your car."

The alternative exit door required them to circle back around the building to the parking lot. They moved as quickly as they could to avoid notice from the reporters still clustered at the main entrance. But one called out as Molly hung the parking pass on Carol's rearview mirror. "Hey, were you in Devon's class?"

Molly merely shook her head as she locked Carol's car again, knowing better than to answer. She certainly wasn't going to cooperate with reporters seeking to break a story about one of her best friends. Fortunately, she had parked right next to the Chrysler, so she hopped into her own car and zoomed out of the lot. Laura and Carol were already gone, as was Bridget.

At this time of day, the Loch Mallaig police station was quiet, but big-haired, bright-lipped receptionist Wilma Guthrie was at her desk. Usually she worked days, but she must have been called in because of the murder investigation. She greeted the small crowd pressing into the reception area, then said, "You know they'll want to talk to Carol by herself." Despite these words, she wore a sympathetic expression on her face.

Harvey put his arm around his wife. "I'm not budging until they release her."

"I'm not talking about you, Harvey," Wilma said, pointedly looking at Molly, Laura, and Bridget. "Spouses can stay as long as they like."

Wilma patted her teased red hair and went back to scrolling on her cell phone.

"We'll wait until Mr. McNab gets here," Molly said. "I want to make sure you're in good hands."

They stood in a tight circle, eyes on the wall clock. Heat steamed from the radiators, causing them to unzip their coats and take off hats and gloves.

The outer door opened and Donal McNab breezed in. Anyone glancing at Donal's rotund build, thinning curly red hair, and friendly crop of freckles would never guess he was a ruthless attorney—until they noticed his sharp, blue eyes. Donal used his seemingly harmless appearance to great effect, often causing his opponents to lower their guard.

"Evening," he said now. "How are you, Carol? Harvey?" He shook their hands, then greeted the others before marching up to the front desk. "Wilma, I'm the attorney of record for Mrs. MacCallan."

Wilma eyed him with respect. "Yes, sir. I'll add you to the file." Her fingers clattered away on the keys.

"You have to give us updates," Molly said, desperately trying to stall. How could she leave one of her best friends to face this without her?

"I will," Carol promised. She met each of their gazes. "I'll be fine with Harvey and Donal here. Go home and get some rest."

Reluctantly, Molly left, with Laura and Bridget right behind her.

"I know there's nothing more I can do here, but I feel as if I should be doing something," Molly said as the trio walked to the parking lot. "I'm not going to be able to sleep a wink until I hear from Carol."

Laura pressed her key fob, making the lights blink on her red Volkswagen Beetle. "Me neither, so I'm going home to work on recipes." She shrugged. "My way of relaxing."

"And I'm going to work on my crime scene map for Marla's death," Bridget said.

Molly was jolted by a sudden memory. "I forgot all about this, but I had a couple of interesting conversations tonight."

"That's right, you did," Laura said. "With Robina and Cole."

Mindful of the cold wind chilling her nose, Molly quickly filled them in. "Dr. Dunbar implied that Robina was taking advantage of Devon's death," she summarized. "And Cole thought he and Marla had a future."

"I see a couple of murder motives there," Bridget said. "You know what? I'm going to map out Devon's death too."

"The question is," Laura said, "did Devon die because we discovered Marla's body? Or is it a separate case?"

"Good question." Molly rubbed her gloves up and down her arms. "Now I'd better get going. I'm freezing."

"Me too," Bridget said with a shiver. "I'll talk to you tomorrow."

Molly's car engine was still warm, so she was able to get underway quickly. As she drove along the quiet Loch Mallaig streets, her thoughts never left Carol. She pictured her friend sitting in the interview room, being questioned by Officer Anderson and probably Chief Thomson.

The officers were likely as unhappy about the situation as everyone else was since Carol and Harvey were well-liked, respected members of the community. Not to mention that the Bakehouse Three had solved many a mystery in conjunction with the local force. Somehow Molly, Laura, and Carol managed to find themselves neck-deep in murder investigations on a regular basis. Now Carol was a person of interest, a suspect even, and Molly would gladly change places with her friend.

Molly found herself getting more and more upset as she drove home. The situation was so unfair. Why had the killer chosen Carol, of all people, to frame? Not only had Carol's chocolates been placed at the scene, but her filling was missing. Why? Had someone duplicated Carol's chocolates using her filling? Or stolen it to make Carol seem even guiltier, as if she'd poisoned it before making her batch, then hidden the evidence?

Either way, Carol was in trouble.

By the time Molly made it through her front door, where a delighted Angus greeted her with enthusiasm, she was on the verge of tears. "Oh, Angus," she said, burying her face in his soft fur. "I'm so worried."

His answer was to lick her on the cheek, which made her laugh. "You silly boy. Do you want a snack?" He wiggled frantically in her arms, eager for a treat.

Molly decided she needed one as well, and after giving him a biscuit, she put on a pan of milk. She'd had plenty of hot cocoa lately, so she decided to make some hot vanilla instead, which was a combination of warm milk, sugar, high-quality vanilla extract, and a dash of cinnamon. A couple of molasses cookies completed the treat.

After curling up on her sofa with her refreshments, she sent Harvey a text. *How's it going?*

Still in with the police, was the answer. *Please pray.*

I am. Molly sent a heartfelt plea heavenward, immediately feeling comforted.

She had finished her hot drink and was absently flipping television channels when Carol called. "How are you?" Molly answered. "What happened?"

"Hold on a second," Carol said. "I'm going to add Laura and Bridget to the call."

Molly waited, her belly churning, while Carol set up the conference call. Angus must have sensed her tension because he hopped up beside her and snuggled against her.

"Are we all here?" Carol asked, and everyone chimed in to say they were on the line. "Okay. First, the good news—I'm not under arrest." The women burst into cheers. Once they settled, Carol went on, "But it was grueling, I'm not going to lie."

"Why are they so focused on you?" Laura asked. "Because of the chocolates?"

"Exactly." Carol inhaled audibly. "The chocolate Devon was holding? It was poisoned."

Again the women exclaimed, but this time with dismay and horror. "With what?" Molly asked, voicing their main question.

"Cyanide," Carol said. "Which is derived from—"

"Apricot pits, the relevant source in this case, I'm guessing," Bridget put in. "Sorry, didn't mean to interrupt."

"Is that why the killer chose your chocolates to use?" Laura asked. "Because you picked the apricot flavor for your filling?"

"I guess so." Carol gave a short, bitter laugh. "Why, oh why, didn't I go with vanilla or coconut? Even strawberry."

"The stolen filling," Molly said. "They wanted it to look like you doctored your candy in advance."

"That's what I think too," Carol said. "Can you imagine me standing in class, making poisonous chocolates? How ridiculous."

"But enough of a distraction to divert attention from the real culprit," Molly said. *And while the police investigate Carol, important evidence could vanish. People could forget important observations.*

"Plus Harvey is still alive," Laura said. "Unless they think you made two batches of filling."

"They floated that theory," Carol said. "But I told them that you three were right there the whole time. I think you would have noticed."

Molly mulled over the situation. "Maybe the killer took your filling and made extra chocolates with poison. Then they decorated the top with a *C* and swapped yours out for theirs."

"Sounds like a good working theory," Bridget said. "Or they

could have injected Carol's chocolates with poison. Either way, they took a huge risk. What if someone besides Devon ate one? Cyanide is extremely deadly."

Deep resolve rose in Molly's chest. "We need to get to the bottom of this. We're going to clear you, Carol."

"We absolutely are," Laura said stoutly. "How did the police leave it?"

"The usual," Carol said. "I have to stay in town and be available if they have more questions. And they said something about searching our home. I told them to go ahead. We have nothing to hide, though they might get pecked if they search the chicken coop."

"Good for you," Molly said. "And meanwhile we'll be investigating the other suspects, like Robina."

"Robina?" Carol asked, her tone curious. "I noticed she stepped right into Devon's slot, no problem."

"Let me tell you about my conversation with her tonight," Molly said. "Laura and Bridget already heard it, so bear with me, you two."

"Tell her about Cole too," Bridget said. "That way we'll all be up to date."

As Molly filled Carol in, Angus sighed and rested his head on Molly's leg. He knew the signs. His person would be on the phone for a while.

"What's the Valentine's special today, Laura?" Molly asked, from the kitchen doorway. "Some customers have asked."

The bakehouse had been mobbed since they'd opened, after a rush to get ready. All three owners had been late that morning, something that hardly ever happened. Carol, especially, had been wiped out after her ordeal with the police the night before.

"Cherry almond," Laura said. She checked the timer. "Coming out in five."

"I'll tell them." Molly let the kitchen door shut. "We have cherry almond Valentine scones today," she announced to her eager customers. "But they're still in the oven. I can get your drinks and then bring you the scones. How's that?"

The customers, a man and woman holding hands, glanced at each other then nodded. "That sounds fine," the woman said. "I'll have a hot vanilla with nutmeg."

Molly had added the new drink to the board as an experiment, and so far, they were selling almost as many vanilla as chocolate hot drinks.

"I'll stick with a large, black coffee," the man said.

"Coming right up," Molly replied.

The bells on the door jingled and Fergus entered. He stamped his snowy boots on the rug, then snatched off his hat. Only Fergus could be so handsome dressed in winter gear. She even adored the rumpled hair he was smoothing.

By the time she served the couple their beverages, he had reached the counter. Carol came through the kitchen door then, holding a tray of heart-shaped cherry almond scones.

Smiling to herself, Molly grabbed one and put it on a plate, then presented it to Fergus. "May I offer you my heart?"

His eyes locked with hers, deep emotion stirring in their depths. He seemed about to say something, but then he simply gave a little headshake. "I'll always take that offer," he said. "And a coffee, please." His brows rose. "Can you come sit with me a minute?"

"Go on," Carol said. "I can handle the counter. Besides, Bridget will be in soon."

Molly delivered the scones to her previous customers, then

grabbed her own drink. By some miracle, a table next to the fireplace was open, so Molly and Fergus sat there.

"What's that you're drinking?" he asked, peering into her mug.

"My newest craze. Hot vanilla." She listed the ingredients.

"I get it," he said. "The hip version of hot milk."

Molly laughed. "That's a great way to put it." She took a sip of the creamy, sweet drink, savoring the vanilla flavor. "Have you heard the latest?" At his questioning expression, she explained, "Carol was almost arrested last night."

"What?" His gaze went to Carol, who was smiling at a customer. "I can't believe it."

"Me neither," Molly said. She took him through the events of the previous evening. "They really don't have anything. It's all circumstantial."

Fergus wore a grim expression. "What do you think of this?" He scrolled on his phone, then placed it so she could see. "It was on television this morning."

Molly recognized the background decoration and furniture. "This was filmed at your resort."

"Robina has a suite there." He sat back, arms folded, so she could concentrate.

Robina was being interviewed remotely by Samantha Glass, a reporter from an entertainment show, so the screen was split. "First we'd like to offer our condolences for the loss of Devon Macintosh," Samantha said, her expression grave. "What a loss to his friends and family, and to his fans."

"It truly is." Robina's brow creased in the perfect display of subdued grief. "And to us, his team, as well. To be honest, we're all still reeling."

"I'll bet." Samantha pursed her lips. "I can't even imagine what you're going through right now. Plus, you're all so far from home."

"We are," Robina said. "In the far northern reaches of Michigan, if you can believe it." She laughed, then added, "But the people are wonderful in Loch Mallaig. So warm and welcoming. Devon went to college here, you know."

Nice plug for Loch Mallaig, Molly thought a little wryly.

"That's right," Samantha said. "At Superior Bay College, where you're filming a chocolate-making class." She paused. "I understand you're stepping in for Devon."

"I am," Robina said. "I didn't want to let the students down." She didn't mention that becoming a substitute also meant stepping in front of the camera as she'd wanted.

"So good of you," the reporter said. "Tell me, what's next for Robina McDonald? I understand that you have an exciting announcement for us tonight."

Robina's eyes lit up and she clasped her hands together in joy. "Yes, I do." She beamed as she said, "I've just gotten word. I'm going to have my own show at last. Robina's Confections is the working title right now. I'll be featuring my own creations, tips, and shortcuts, as well as candy recipes from around the world."

Molly stopped the video as the reporter began to gush. "Wow. Do you think this was a coincidence?"

Fergus pressed his lips together. "Maybe." He lowered his voice. "Or a motive. Going by what she said, I gather she's wanted her own show for a while. Perhaps Devon was standing in her way."

"Something to check into, that's for sure," Molly said.

Bridget emerged from the kitchen and bustled over to Molly's table with an electronic tablet. "Sorry to interrupt, but I've been doing some research."

Molly exchanged an amused glance with Fergus before pushing out a chair. "Please join us."

The young woman perched on the chair. "You know they said Devon was poisoned with cyanide."

"Molly filled me in," Fergus said. "It's not exactly something you buy at the store."

"And it's very, very deadly," Bridget said. "Common sources are pesticides and herbicides, and it's released in cigarette smoke and other fires, particularly when burning synthetic materials like plastic."

"I did not know that," Molly said.

"But we're not concerned with any of those sources," Bridget said, and Molly was impressed by her professionalism. She'd be an excellent forensic scientist someday—and with graduation approaching, that day could be soon. "The police aren't either. Because Carol used apricots in her filling, they're searching for apricot stones, specifically the kernels inside. They contain a toxin called amygdalin, which converts to cyanide when it's consumed. Did you know that eating only three of those can be dangerous?" She showed a picture on the tablet screen, and Molly noticed how closely the kernels resembled almonds. "Sometimes it's by accident."

"Who would eat the pits on purpose?" Fergus asked. "I've never been tempted in the least."

"Some people think they might cure cancer," Bridget said. "There have been some experimental treatments." She shook her head. "But Devon didn't have cancer, and he wasn't voluntarily eating the kernels. I think someone extracted the poison and made a concentrate, which they then injected into the candy. Another option is that they added it to Carol's filling and made fresh chocolates that matched hers."

"How would someone do that?" Fergus asked. "It doesn't sound like it would be that simple."

Bridget smiled as she showed them a website. "I found out how through a simple search. See? You can extract the cyanide via a scientific process."

Molly's heart gave a jolt. "Bridget, you shouldn't be researching that. What if they see your browsing history and think—"

"That I did it?" Bridget shook her head. "No worries. I'm searching after the fact."

Fergus eyed Bridget with admiration. "You are clever. So now the police need to find out who had whole apricots and the ability to do the extraction."

Once again Molly thought of Blane. "I know someone who buys apricots all the time." She used her own phone to bring up Blane's website. "See? He offers chocolate-dipped apricots."

"Wouldn't he use dried ones?" Fergus inquired. "Surely he buys them already processed."

Molly studied the website more closely. "It says that he starts with fresh fruit from small farms, so he must dry them himself. I know some of the dried fruit you buy uses sulfur in the process. He probably wanted to avoid that."

"Would he have the knowledge to make the poison?" Fergus asked. "Shouldn't we consider someone who is a food scientist?"

Without him saying the name, Molly understood. "You mean Dr. Dunbar. She certainly has a scientific background."

"And access to equipment," Bridget said. "But look at this article." She showed them another site. "This man gave himself cyanide poisoning with a homemade apricot extract."

Heads together, Molly and Fergus skimmed the article. "So specialized knowledge isn't essential," Molly said. "This is all great work, Bridget. But it doesn't positively narrow down our suspects."

"I know," Bridget said with a sigh. "It's frustrating. Whoever poisoned Devon had access to Carol's filling, which was in the walk-in refrigerator attached to the classroom. So Robina, Cole, Dr. Dunbar, or Blane could have grabbed it."

"It's not locked?" Fergus asked. "That surprises me."

"Actually it is, with a combination lock," Bridget said. "They've all been helping with Devon's show, though, so I'm sure they know the combo."

"Yes, all four had the perfect excuse to go into the walk-in," Molly said. "And they could have easily taken Carol's chocolates that had been set aside for judging and injected the poison. Or they could have seen Carol's design in class and made a copy."

"Are the police investigating anyone else?" Fergus asked. "Or just Carol?"

Molly drank the rest of her hot vanilla, which was actually cold now. "I have no idea. But maybe I should pay Chief Thomson a visit later today. The longer they wait, the more time the killer has to get rid of evidence."

"It sounds like other people had means, motive, and opportunity," Fergus said. "The evidence against Carol is purely circumstantial."

"I agree," Molly said. "She was framed."

"Can I go with you to see the chief?" Bridget asked, clasping her hands in entreaty. "Pretty please?"

"I don't see why not," Molly agreed. "I've met with him plenty of times. And he's been pretty good about me sticking my nose in."

"He should be," Fergus said. "You ladies have been invaluable to his department."

"I appreciate you saying that, Fergus," Molly said. "It's not like we try to get involved."

Fergus nodded toward Molly's empty mug. "I should let you get back to work. Don't forget we have a performance tonight with The Leaping Lowlanders."

Molly clapped a hand to her forehead. "I forgot all about it. I know what I'm doing after I visit Chief Thomson. Practicing."

"Why don't I meet you here?" Fergus suggested. "We can run through the numbers together. I'll bring takeout from the resort for dinner."

"Perfect," Molly said. "I hadn't even thought about dinner, and I hate to play on an empty stomach."

Fergus stood. "You know, Bridget, I think Neil might come watch the performance tonight."

"Really?" Bridget's cheeks flushed, complementing the raspberry streak in her hair. She blinked a few times, as if trying to bat away the eagerness in her voice. "I mean, that's cool." Then she scurried back to the kitchen.

Molly and Fergus exchanged glances, and Fergus wiggled his eyebrows. Molly suppressed a grin. Apparently Cupid was hard at work in Loch Mallaig this Valentine's Day.

"The chief can see us if we go right now," Molly told Bridget as she disconnected the call. They were in the middle of cleaning up after the bakehouse closed. "But I hate to leave you two stuck with everything," she said to Carol and Laura.

"Go ahead," Carol said as she loaded the dishwasher. "We can do the rest with no problem."

"Don't do everything," Molly said. "When I come back, I'll put away the clean dishes."

"And I'll mop the floors," Bridget said.

"Deal," Laura said as she wiped down the kitchen counters. "I'll see you both at the Lowlanders performance."

Molly rolled her eyes. "Thank goodness Fergus is coming by to practice with me. I haven't picked up my bagpipes for weeks."

"Hopefully you two will get around to practicing," Carol said with a cheeky smile. At Molly's frown, she laughed. "Just teasing. You and Fergus always have so much to talk about."

"True," Molly said, but her frown remained. "You know, I've been getting an odd vibe from Fergus now and then. He's been a little distant."

"I wouldn't worry about it," Carol said quickly. "I'm sure he has a lot on his mind."

"Agreed," Laura said. "Anyone with eyes can see that he's head over heels for you."

"You think?" Molly felt reassured. If something was really wrong, she could count on Carol and Laura to tell her, couldn't she? "All right. I'm out of here. See you later."

Molly and Bridget went over to the police station together in Molly's Honda Fit. "Wow, town sure is busy," Bridget said as they drove. "So many people around."

"Apparently Devon's death didn't scare them away," Molly said, stopping to let a group of pedestrians cross the street.

"Or Marla's. The school had to block off the area where she was found."

"Ugh. I wonder what's going on with that investigation."

"Why don't we ask Chief Thomson? Judging by the news, Devon's death pushed Marla's story to the back burner."

"I suppose that makes sense," Molly said. "Marla is a cold case, so that initial window of investigation isn't as pressing. There's no fresh evidence to preserve. I'm sure they'll focus more on her soon."

"Once they figure out who killed Devon, I bet." Bridget tapped her gloved fingers on the armrest. "My mind keeps whirling like a hamster on a wheel, rotating through all the suspects and coming to no definite conclusion."

Molly signaled for the turn into the town hall parking lot. "I know the feeling," she said. Every investigation seemed to be like that, a complete muddle before something broke and the solution became obvious. She prayed that would happen again—and soon, to relieve poor Carol's mind.

Wilma greeted them as they walked in, then asked, "Here to see the chief? He said he had an appointment."

"That's us," Molly said, unzipping her coat. "How are you today?"

The receptionist made a face. "Tired. Working overtime this week and probably next." But then she shrugged. "Sorry. Didn't mean to complain. I love my job."

"Glad to hear that," Chief Thomson said, coming up behind Wilma.

Wilma jumped, a hand to her chest. "Oh, chief. You surprised me."

"Sorry." Chief Thomson winked at Molly and Bridget. "Please come in, ladies." As they followed him into the main part of the station, he said, "We're all working a lot of hours right now between the Winter Faire and now these two cases. Wilma's not the only one who's tired."

"I'll bet," Molly said. "Bridget and I were noticing how busy it is in town. We have so many visitors right now."

Once in his office, Chief Thomson indicated they should sit down in the visitor chairs. "It's a good thing for Loch Mallaig. But we've had to increase patrols as well as attend events."

"And now you have two murder cases," Molly said. "That's why I—we—wanted to see you." She threw Bridget an encouraging smile, noticing that the college student appeared nervous. That was perfectly normal, since many people were uneasy when talking to the police. Molly had also felt that way once but now, for better or worse, she was used to such circumstances.

The chief swiveled in his chair, which squeaked. "I gathered as much," he said, a faint smile playing around his lips before he put up a hand. "One topic that is off-limits is Carol MacCallan. I know you're good friends with her, but I can't discuss her case." His expression grew grim. "It's up to the prosecutor now."

12

Molly's heart sank at the chief's mention of the prosecutor. Yes, the police investigated and gathered evidence, but the prosecutor decided whether or not to press charges. Was the chief implying that Carol's arrest was imminent? Even thinking that made Molly shiver in dismay.

"Do you mean—" Molly blurted, only to be met with a firm headshake from the chief to reassert his previous statement. "I'm sorry," she said quickly. The main reason they were here, she reminded herself, was to tell the chief all they'd gleaned in their own investigation, not pry into the status of Carol's case or make pleas on her behalf.

Molly took a moment to gather her thoughts, then finally said, "All right. We've learned some things and made some connections that I think you'll find interesting."

Between Molly and Bridget, they went through the list of suspects, detailing the motive, means, and opportunity that each had.

"One thing I haven't figured out yet," Molly said next, "is whether Devon's murder is related to Marla Bannerman's death. All of our suspects knew Marla and in fact were quite close with her."

Bridget edged forward on her seat. "Should I show the chief my map?" she asked Molly. When Molly nodded, Bridget took out the document and placed it on the desk. "This shows the location of key sites related to Marla's death."

"As you know, Bridget is training to become a forensic scientist," Molly said. "And investigate crime scenes."

"This is a great approach," the chief said, his gaze roaming over the map. "Very professional."

"You probably know all this," Molly said, not wanting to imply that the chief's investigation was less than thorough, "but we learned some interesting things from Dr. Pryde, who used to be Marla's professor."

Bridget made a face. "I'm part of the new generation of students he's torturing." At the chief's surprised expression, she added, "I'm kidding."

Between Molly and Bridget, they shared what Dr. Pryde had said about Marla's paper being plagiarized. They showed the chief the student newspaper articles hinting at a cheating scandal. Molly also told him what she knew about Marla's personal relationships, namely that she had been dating Cole. She added that Blane had said Marla had her eye on Devon, which gave Cole a motive.

"Come to think of it, Cole might have held a grudge against Devon all this time," Molly said. "In any event, I have the feeling that the discovery of Marla's body has now triggered a chain reaction."

"You could be right," Chief Thomson admitted, rubbing his chin thoughtfully.

"Devon's death could also be related to something that's happening now," Molly said. "Namely his show."

"There are a lot of possible motives," the chief said. "That's why we have to focus on the evidence, which is cut and dried, factual."

Like the chocolates bearing Carol's symbol. Molly swallowed hard. "We understand, chief," she said, rising from her seat. "Thanks for listening."

At five o'clock, Fergus arrived at Molly's door with his bagpipes case over his shoulder and two paper sacks in his arms.

"Something smells good," Molly said, tugging him forward. Angus immediately danced around in excitement at their guest's feet. "Angus thinks so too."

"Beef burgundy," Fergus explained as he set the sacks on the kitchen table and pulled out containers. "Handmade egg noodles and steamed broccoli. Fresh dinner rolls. And, last but not least, apple crumble." He raised an insulated bag. "With ice cream of course."

Molly took the ice cream from him. "I'll put this in the freezer."

They served up the meal, then sat at the table to eat. "I figured we needed a hot, hearty meal if we're going to spend the evening outside," Fergus said.

"Absolutely," Molly agreed, scooping up a forkful of noodles, beef, and gravy. "We need fuel for our personal furnaces."

Angus, who'd already had his dinner, was under the table, draped over Fergus's feet. "Is he coming with us?" Fergus asked.

"I think he'd better stay here," she said, dropping her voice to a whisper. "If we weren't performing, I'd bring him."

Fergus chuckled. "Worried he'll hear you?" he whispered back.

"Yes," Molly said. "He seems to understand everything I say." Angus grunted, and they both laughed. "See what I mean?"

During dinner, they kept the topics light. Molly talked about the success of Laura's Valentine's scones. Fergus gave her updates about the resort, which continued to be at full capacity. "I'm so thankful for Neil," he said. "At this point, I could step away entirely and the resort would be fine." His face creased in a smile. "Not that I'm planning to go anywhere for a while."

"Me neither," Molly said. "I love my business." She'd always been a doer, and the idea of retiring didn't appeal as of yet.

"I could use a vacation, though," Fergus mused. "How about you?"

"The three of us have talked about each taking off at different times,"

Molly said. "A few days at a time is easy enough, but it gets harder the longer we want to take. The toughest issue is picking up the slack for Laura so she can take a long trip. She's our star baker."

"I get that," Fergus said. "It takes some planning, that's all. And maybe she could go during the slower times."

Molly speared her last bright-green broccoli crown. "If we ever get any."

They both chuckled. Loch Mallaig's marketing efforts had been so successful that the small town was busy year-round.

"We're a victim of our success," Fergus said. "But I'll take it over the opposite."

"Hear, hear," Molly said. "Ready for dessert?"

After enjoying the apple crumble and clearing up the kitchen, Molly and Fergus adjourned to the den. They ran through the numbers they'd be playing later when The Leaping Lowlanders skated.

"I'm so glad we did this," Molly said after they finished the set. "I was really rusty." She'd squeaked and squawked far more than she liked.

"It sounded better than you think. We're always more critical of our own playing than others are." Fergus began to take apart his bagpipes. "It's fun practicing with you. We should do it more often."

"Agreed," Molly said. She studied him as he carefully stowed the instrument. "Everything is way more fun with you," she blurted, then immediately felt her face flush.

He glanced up, his eyes warm with affection. "That's how I feel. It doesn't matter what we're doing—it's better when I do it with you." Angus, who had been listening to them practice, gave a yip, then trotted over for a pat. "Yes, you too, buddy."

Soon they were on their way to the performance, which was being held on the loch. Volunteers had worked hard to keep the ice clear for skating and iceboat races. Tonight, torches ringed the skating area, casting a magical glow over the scene.

Molly spotted Bridget among the skate-clad dancers on the ice, dressed in her usual tartan kilt but with thick wool stockings, a short wool jacket, and white hat and mittens. Since the focus would be on the Lowlanders tonight, Molly and the other Piping Yoopers were wearing regular outdoor clothing and snow boots.

"They're renting skates," Fergus observed as they passed by a couple of changing huts. A booth nearby offered skates for a reasonable fee. "Want to take a spin after?"

Molly thought about his offer, debating between trying something fun and challenging or rushing home and getting warm. On a cold night like this, it was definitely a toss-up. But when she saw his eager expression, she found herself agreeing. "All right. Let's do it. But I'm warning you, I haven't skated for a long time. You'll have to hold me up."

"No problem." Fergus halted in front of the booth. "I'd like to reserve two pairs of skates for later." He told the attendant the sizes, and she directed them to pick out their own pairs. Molly chose a pretty white pair with pink laces.

That business concluded, they joined the rest of The Piping Yoopers on the shore. "Fergus, Molly," Alastair greeted them. "So glad you could make it." He gestured for them to take their places in the troupe.

Molly's spot was next to Greer. "You made it," Molly said. She'd thought that the officer might be too busy with the murder cases.

"I did," Greer said. "I told the chief I needed a break. And playing clears my head."

Molly hoped it would clear hers as well. While they waited for the signal to start, she studied the crowd of onlookers, which was growing by the moment. Noticing Harvey's tartan cap, she saw Carol and Laura standing next to him and waved. Neil stood nearby with a few friends Molly recognized from around town. Dr. Dunbar wove her way through the throng, right to the front. A short distance away stood

Robina and Blane, and Cole was filming the event, likely gathering more background material for the show.

Dallis Witherspoon, leader of The Leaping Lowlanders, skated forward, holding a microphone. Alastair gave the bagpipers a signal, and they played a jaunty fragment of music to alert the audience.

"Good evening," Dallis said. "Welcome to Follies on Ice, a special performance from The Leaping Lowlanders." Behind him, the dance troupe waved. The crowd clapped loudly in welcome.

Dallis gave a few more comments about the upcoming performance, and then it commenced. Molly had to concentrate on her playing, but she was able to take in brief glimpses of the dancers. They'd done a remarkable job translating their traditional Scottish dances to ice, and they were sheer poetry in motion, twirling and jumping, circling and waltzing. Molly was in awe of their grace and talent.

The audience loved it too, breaking into cheers and applause between each number. "This might have to be a regular event," Greer whispered to Molly.

"Absolutely," Molly agreed. "I love it." She was glad that Cole was filming the event so she could watch it later without the distraction of playing the bagpipes.

They concluded the performance with a rousing rendition of "Scotland the Brave" before the Lowlanders took bows and filed off the ice.

"That was fantastic," Carol said, rushing up to join Molly and Fergus, who were packing away their bagpipes.

"I feel like dancing myself," Harvey said from behind her. He tipped his head toward his wife. "I convinced this one that we need to rent skates."

"Laura's already out there," Carol said. She pointed to where Laura and Trent were easing out into the skating area.

"We rented skates too," Molly said. "We'll see you on the ice."

Molly and Fergus went to pick up their skates, and the attendant offered to watch their bagpipes for them. "I'll be here until ten," she said.

"That's plenty of time," Molly said, thinking she might survive an hour on the ice.

She picked up her skates and popped into one of the huts, where she changed out of her boots. She made sure to lace the skates tightly, as she'd been instructed in the past.

"Fergus?" she called when she was ready, steadying herself on the door casings. She felt like a bumbling fawn on a slick surface.

"I'm here," he said, gliding along in the snow. He crooked an elbow. "Take my arm, milady."

With a laugh, she complied, and they shuffled over to the loch, Fergus steadying her when she slipped. "Whoops," she said. "Please tell me this is like riding a bike."

"It definitely is," Fergus said. "But it can take a bit to get comfortable."

Out on the loch, they moved in unison, Fergus's arm around her waist and her hand firmly gripped in his other hand. She copied his movements—left, right, left, right—gradually building speed as she got used to balancing on a narrow metal blade.

Other couples glided by, some showing off with spins and twirls. But soon Molly and Fergus were keeping up and she was comfortable enough to look around. It was beautiful out here, the carnival lights on the shore, stars twinkling in the inky sky above. Jaunty music played over the speaker system, and other skaters laughed and shouted in joy.

Fergus's arm tightened around her waist. "How are you doing?"

"I'm loving this. Why don't we do it more often?"

"We can," he said. "I'm clearing a skating area at the resort too, so we can have lunch and go sometime soon."

"That sounds lovely," Molly said.

"Ready to try a spin?" Fergus asked. "I'm going to let you go out, then twirl back into my arms."

Molly's heart thumped, both at the suggestion of trying something new and unfamiliar and at the thought of being in his arms. It was a perfect metaphor for her relationship with him—the excitement of the new mingled with the safety and warmth of his embrace.

"All right, I'm ready," she said.

Still holding her hand, he took his arm away from her shoulders. The distance between them grew. At his signal, Molly rotated on the spot as if they were on the dance floor, allowing their gripped hands to rise above her head as she twirled. Then she finally reached him, cocooned again in the warmth of his grip.

"That was awesome," she said, laughing up into his face. "And you know what? It was also a perfect finale to this skating session. If we don't quit while we're ahead, I might not be able to walk tomorrow."

"We wouldn't want that," Fergus said. "Let's go in."

Together they skated to the shore, where Fergus helped Molly cross the snow to the changing hut. She slipped inside to change into her boots, which she'd placed along the wall.

Thanks to a knot in the laces, the process took longer than she anticipated. Finally the skates were off and her feet felt as if they breathed a sigh of relief as she slipped on the roomier snow boots. She put her gloves back on and picked up the skates to return them.

"Fergus?" Molly called as she stepped outside. The lighting was poor back here, forcing her to squint into the darkness. He must have gone to another hut to change, or maybe he was already waiting for her at the rental booth.

Something rustled behind her. Before she could turn to see what it was, Molly was seized in an iron grip. A broad, gloved hand went across her mouth—a hand that smelled of chocolate.

"Butt out," came a hoarse whisper. "Mind your own business—or else."

13

Molly fought, shoving against her captor's arms in an attempt to break his grip on her. She also lifted her foot and slammed it down, trying to stomp on his foot, having read that the instep was an especially sensitive place.

With a muffled grunt, the attacker shoved Molly forward. She landed on her knees in the deep snow as footsteps thudded away behind her. The skates soared away and landed in a puff of snow.

"Molly." Fergus came around the corner of the hut. "What are you doing on the ground?"

"Someone pushed me and I fell." She grabbed his extended hand and stood, testing to see how bruised her knees were. Her left one stung, but the right was okay.

"Pushed you?" Fergus sounded appalled. "Who did that? And why?"

"I don't know," Molly said, brushing off her pants. "I didn't see him. When I came out of the changing room, someone grabbed me." She demonstrated how he'd clapped a hand across her mouth. "He said, 'Butt out. Mind your own business—or else.' I stomped on his foot and he gave me a shove, then he ran off."

Anger flashed in Fergus's eyes. "Which way did he go?"

Molly pointed. "But like I said, I didn't see him. The only thing I remember is that his glove smelled like chocolate."

"Got it." Fergus took off running in the direction Molly had indicated.

Molly groaned. "Fergus," she called. "I'm sure he's gone." He didn't come back, so she settled for yelling, "Be careful!"

"What's going on?" Carol and Laura came around the corner of the hut. "We heard you shouting."

Molly began to hunt for the skates. "Someone accosted me and Fergus is trying to catch him." She sensed rather than saw her friends exchange looks.

"What do you mean someone accosted you?" Carol asked.

"It's okay," Molly said. "I'm not hurt. Someone grabbed me and gave me a warning. Told me to butt out. I stomped on his foot and he ran off." She spotted a skate-size depression in the snow. "Ah, here they are." She grabbed the skates and brushed them off.

Laura stepped forward. "Are you sure you're okay? You're awfully blasé about this."

"I'm fine," Molly said, though her laugh sounded brittle even to her own ears. "Seriously. I mean, I was pretty scared when he grabbed me, but it was all over in moments."

Carol slung an arm around Molly's shoulders. "Let's go get a hot drink while we wait for Fergus."

"All right," Molly said. "After I return these skates."

They went to the rental booth first, where Molly gave the attendant her skates and retrieved her bagpipes. Another booth nearby was selling hot drinks, so they went there next. Instead of hot cocoa, Molly decided on mulled cider.

They found Harvey and Trent sipping from their own to-go cups nearby. "You'll never believe it," Carol told them. "Someone attacked Molly."

Both men exclaimed in alarm. "Where did he go?" Harvey demanded, tossing his cup into a trash can.

"Fergus is already chasing him," Molly said. "But it won't do any good. The only detail I have is that his glove smelled like chocolate." She couldn't help herself. She burst out laughing. "I can't wait to tell the police my big clue." The laughter turned into tears.

"I've been expecting this," Carol said, hugging Molly again. "Delayed reaction."

"I need to go find the officer on duty," Harvey said to Trent. "Want to stay here and guard the women?"

Trent crossed his arms, a determined set to his jaw. "You bet I will."

Carol rolled her eyes as her husband set off, arms swinging. "As if anyone will bother us here, in this crowd."

"I love how protective he is," Molly said with a sniff. "So dependable."

Her friend softened. "Yes, he is. And so is yours." She handed Molly a fresh tissue.

Harvey soon returned with Officer Dalziel Murdoch in tow. As a younger officer in the department, twentysomething Officer Murdoch could be underestimated due to his slight stature and occasionally anxious demeanor, but he was as sharp as they came.

"How are you doing, Mrs. Ferris?" Officer Murdoch asked.

"I'm okay," Molly said. "A little shaken up, that's all."

"Feel up to telling me what happened?" At Molly's nod, the officer said, "Okay. Take me through it from the top. Where were you?"

Molly launched into her tale.

When she paused for breath, Laura said, "Here comes Fergus."

"Fergus went to try to catch the guy who attacked me," Molly explained to Officer Murdoch.

"Any luck?" Murdoch asked Fergus as he joined them.

Fergus shook his head. "I didn't see anyone running away. He probably went a different direction and blended into the crowd." He moved closer to Molly. "Are you okay, sweetheart?"

Molly attempted a smile. "Yeah, I'm fine. You missed my breakdown."

"Which was perfectly understandable," Carol added. "She was in shock," she told Fergus. "Laughing and crying—the whole bit."

Fergus gathered Molly into a hug. "From now on, I'm going to be looking for guys with gloves that smell like chocolate." The image that statement evoked made Molly laugh again, but this time tears didn't follow.

"What's this about his gloves?" Officer Murdoch asked Molly.

Once Molly had recounted her experience, including the detail of the chocolate-scented gloves, Officer Murdoch promised to file a report and left.

Laura handed Molly her cider. "It's probably cold."

Molly took a sip. "No, it's okay."

"Ready to head home?" Fergus asked.

"More than ready," Molly said. Besides her banged knee, her other muscles were beginning to feel sore from skating. A hot bath and a good night's sleep would set her right.

Once she finished her cider, Fergus and Molly said good night to their friends and walked back to the bakehouse, Fergus insisting on carrying both sets of bagpipes. He'd even offered to go get his car, but Molly told him that she preferred to keep moving. Still, she was hobbling by the time they climbed the stairs to her apartment.

"Do you want to come in?" she asked. Eager for her hot bath, she wasn't entirely disappointed when he shook his head.

"I'm going to let you get a good night's rest," Fergus said, setting down her bagpipes bag. In the glow of the overhead bulb, she saw a shadow cross his face. "Molly," he began, his voice growing thick. He cleared his throat. "I'm glad you're okay. It scared me to think that you might not have been. You were probably accosted by a murderer, and I wasn't there to protect you."

"Oh, Fergus," Molly said. His protectiveness warmed her. "I'm all right."

"That isn't the point," Fergus said, his eyes haunted. "I don't want to lose you. In fact—" A tense silence fell, and Molly sensed he was grappling with something he wanted to say. But Angus barking inside the apartment shattered the moment.

What had he been about to say? Molly wished she knew—or dared to ask. Pressing him felt wrong. "See you tomorrow?" she said instead. "I'm going over to watch the dogsled races if you want to join me." She'd arranged with Carol and Laura to take turns slipping over to the faire.

"I'll let you know," he said, dropping a kiss on her forehead. Was it her imagination or was his hug tighter than usual? "Don't go anywhere alone, okay? Stay in view of the crowds."

"I will," Molly promised. She unlocked the door and picked up her bagpipes. "Believe me, I have no interest in another encounter with whoever that was."

"Big news," Bridget sang out when she entered the bakehouse kitchen the next morning. "You will be flabbergasted." She peeled off her coat and hat and hung them on a peg. "Isn't that the funniest word?"

"If you don't hurry up and spit it out, you'll hear some funny words from me." Carol poured Bridget a mug of coffee and fixed it the way she preferred.

After changing out of her boots into shoes, Bridget came over to pick up the mug. She sipped and smiled. "This is perfect. Thanks." After a second drink, she said, "Get this. Robina McDonald went to Superior Bay College at the same time as everyone else. She was a freshman their senior year."

"Get out." Laura paused while measuring dry ingredients for her Valentine scones. Today's new creation featured a strawberry rhubarb filling with a cream cheese glaze. "I didn't know that."

"I assumed she was from the San Francisco area because she was Devon's assistant," Carol said. "Bad of me."

"Same here," Molly admitted. "I didn't even think to research her background for a connection."

Bridget found a stool and perched. "It's not mentioned in her bio, which I checked out when I signed up for the chocolate class. I was curious about how someone got to be a television star's assistant."

"It does sound like a cool job," Molly said. *Until your boss gets murdered.* "How did you find out she was a student here?"

"I decided to dig a little deeper," Bridget said. "Actually, I combed her social media pages. When she posted about filming at Superior Bay, one of her friends said, 'Isn't that where you used to go?' Robina wrote back, 'Only for freshman year. Then I transferred.' She graduated from a fancy culinary school in Vermont."

"So she never bothered to mention Superior Bay." Carol loaded a basket with wrapped day-old baked goods. "I probably wouldn't either."

Laura began to chop thawed strawberries. "The big question is, did she know Marla? Or any of the others?"

"Good question," Molly said. "And I wonder if the chief knows she attended Superior Bay." If she'd hidden it, the question would be why.

Bridget slid off the stool. "Think I should call him?" She appeared to be equally thrilled and scared at the idea.

"Why not?" Carol shrugged one shoulder. "You're trying to help. And cases have been solved with less."

The young woman squared her shoulders. "I'll do it. Be right back." She marched over to her coat and pulled out her cell phone, then she slipped into the front room to make the call. She returned a few minutes later.

"What did he say?" Molly asked.

"I had to leave a message." Bridget cringed. "Wilma was very skeptical about the whole thing, I could tell. I just told her that Robina, Devon's assistant, went to college here as a freshman, the same year Marla died."

Laura pursed her lips. "Don't worry about it. It's not her call whether or not it's important." She nodded toward the pantry. "Bridget, can you get me a large jar of the rhubarb preserves?"

"Right away." Bridget crossed the kitchen to the storeroom.

"Are you still okay with me going to the faire later this morning?" Molly asked. She planned to combine Angus's walk with watching snowmobile and dogsled events.

"I am," Carol said. "Have at it."

"Fine by me," Laura agreed. "How about we go shopping after we close? I really need to get a dress for Valentine's Day. And if Happily Ever After doesn't have something, I need to make time to go to Marquette." She smiled wryly. "I don't think Trent has seen me in a dress yet."

"He's in for a treat, then," Molly said. "I'm in." She picked up a tray of mugs.

"Same here," Carol said, then peered at Molly. "How's your knee? Are you up to working behind the counter?"

Molly flexed her leg. She still had a bruise, but it was barely noticeable. As for the encounter with her assailant, she was trying not to think about it. "I'm fine. Hot bath, over-the-counter painkillers, good night's sleep. I'm not even sore from skating, which is a miracle."

"I hear you," Carol said with a chuckle. "Poor Harvey was moaning and groaning this morning. Fishing doesn't utilize quite the same muscles as skating."

"Sounds like he needs to join you for Pilates one of these days," Laura said. "I'd pay to see him try to keep up with you."

Everyone laughed, then went about their tasks as they prepared to open for the day. Midmorning, after the initial rush and Hamish's arrival, Molly went upstairs to get ready for her outing. She changed into layers and fastened a plaid coat on Angus since today's temperatures were well below freezing.

"It's a chilly one, Angus," she told him. "But at least the sun is shining." Fergus had sent a text to say he couldn't make it, so Molly and Angus would be on their own today.

The walk over to the park was brisk but bearable since there was practically no wind. Quite a crowd had gathered, undeterred by the weather. Molly went over to the dogsled races first, which were using the same course she'd done on snowshoes.

Teams of dogs were harnessed and ready to go, with their owners making last-minute adjustments. "How would you like to do that, Angus?" Molly asked, smiling at the thought of her intrepid Scottie pulling a sled. He yipped and tugged on the leash to get closer to his fellow canines.

A parka-clad man holding a video camera was talking to one of the racers. Molly recognized Cole and figured he must be here to film the events for the show. Molly thought about their last conversation. Maybe at some point today she could talk to him again—in private, unlike the other night with the students and other suspects listening in.

As they had during the snowshoe race, teams went out in waves, with starting and finishing times recorded. A tingle went up Molly's spine as the leaders gave their teams the signal to move and the dogs lunged forward, harness bells jingling.

"Quite the sight, isn't it?" Greer said, joining Molly. She was in uniform, so on duty or on her way to the station.

"I love it," Molly said. "It's like something you'd see up in the Yukon."

"Or in a movie," Greer said with enthusiasm. "I'd love to try mushing someday." Then her brows drew together. "How are you this morning, Molly? I heard about the attack last night."

Molly caught movement out of the corner of her eye. Cole was a couple of feet away, filming the onlookers and their reactions. She waited until he moved off before saying, "I'm okay. I fell onto my knees after he pushed me, so I'm sore from that, but that's all."

Greer winced. "I'm sorry to hear that."

"I wish I'd seen more details," Molly said. "It's going to be impossible to identify him." She wasn't even sure about his height or weight. He'd been strong, though.

"Unfortunately you're correct about that. One thing seems clear to me, though."

"What's that?" Molly asked after a moment.

The officer leaned close and whispered, "Carol didn't do it," then briskly moved off through the crowd.

Well, at least one member of the force supported Molly's theory that Carol had been framed. "Everything has an upside, right, Angus?"

Next Molly and Angus made their way to the snowmobile area, where snowmobiles were buzzing around a rolling course performing jumps and stunts. Molly sucked in a breath as one helmeted rider launched off a big jump and "really got some air," as fans called it.

"Cool." Cole had come to stand beside her, and he was staring through his viewfinder at the course. "They're almost ready for the X Games."

Is he following me? No, it couldn't be. There wasn't much to see right now at the sled races, so it made sense that Cole had wandered over here. Besides, she'd hoped to talk to him, and now the opportunity had presented itself.

"Acting crazy on snowmobiles is a sport?" Molly asked. She'd thought they were only having fun pushing their machines to the limit.

"It sure is," Cole said, lowering the camera as the rider finished the course. "I'm getting some great clips."

"Filler for the chocolate show?" Molly asked.

"That and so much more." Cole cracked a grin. Molly noticed how attractive he was when he smiled, in a boy-next-door way. "I can sell whatever I don't use on the show to other outlets. Local news stations, travel shows, sports shows, even the Loch Mallaig business bureau."

"They don't have much of a budget, I'm afraid," Molly said.

Cole shrugged. "Not surprising." He held the camera to his eye again as another racer burst onto the course. "But I usually sell most of my stuff sooner or later."

He must be pretty good, then. But still, Devon's show had provided regular work. She waited for him to stop filming and then asked, "Are you going to be shooting Robina's new show?"

His lip curled. "Doubt it. She's got some pretty big ideas all of a sudden. I'm not well-known enough, she said."

"Yikes," Molly said. "That's gratitude for you."

Cole scowled. "No kidding. But I wouldn't want to work with her anyway." He swallowed visibly, Adam's apple bobbing. "I think she had something to do with Devon's death."

14

"What?" Molly's exclamation was a little too loud. She glanced around, hoping no one had heard. She lowered her voice to a whisper. "Seriously, Cole, you think she did it?"

He shifted from foot to foot uneasily. "I don't want to go that far. But she was definitely unhappy working with him."

Molly decided to take a more indirect route in questioning him. "Was he difficult to work with? I've heard some stars are."

Cole gazed into space, gnawing at his lip. "No, Devon was okay. Oh, he had his vision for things and insisted you follow it, but who doesn't?"

"Understandable," Molly murmured. She remembered something she'd overheard. "Did he let Robina contribute?"

"He sure did. All the time. He even sought out her opinion, had her help him test new candy. I think where it got touchy was when it came to giving credit." His eyes were knowing. "Somehow Devon was always listed as the recipe author. And when he talked about his recipes, he never mentioned how she'd helped him develop them."

"I can see how that might upset her," Molly said.

Cole reached for his wool cap, rearranging it on his head. "That it did. She got super mad sometimes. Like the day he died. I heard her screaming that she was going to 'get Devon.'"

Molly's pulse leaped. Had Robina killed her boss? She sounded like she had been angry enough. "Have you told the police?"

He shrugged, uncomfortable. "Think I should? I hate to rat someone out—"

"Cole." Molly injected as much authority as she could into her voice. "Devon was murdered. If you know anything that might shine some light on what happened, you need to go to the police." When he still appeared uncertain, she added, "Today."

His response was to stare into space again. A moment later, when another contestant roared onto the course, he moved away to film the action. Molly exhaled. She sincerely hoped he would do as she suggested. She really couldn't go to the police herself about this conversation since it was hearsay. If she'd heard Robina ranting and raving, that would be another thing.

As she and Angus watched the snowmobiler go through his tricks, she realized something. According to Blane, Devon had stolen his family recipes and used them without credit—and now it sounded like he had done the same thing to Robina. *What nerve, using other people's creativity and talent to get ahead.* What would it have hurt to give credit where it was due? Devon had been charming, personable, and talented, but he'd also been a thief.

And now he was dead and Robina had her own show. She'd certainly landed on her feet.

Angus pulled at the leash, restless, and Molly decided to walk back to the dogsled race, where the first contestants were coming in.

If only she could learn something that would eliminate one of the suspects. Dr. Dunbar, Blane, Cole, and Robina—all were still front-runners. All she was sure of was that the person who grabbed her last night had been a man, so it wasn't Dr. Dunbar or Robina—unless one of them had hired someone.

Molly growled, and Angus peered up at her in confusion. "Sorry, boy. I'm frustrated, that's all." She sighed and tried to enjoy the rest of her outing, hoping that the clues and suspicions swirling in her mind might make sense of themselves if she didn't actively think about them. She didn't expect it to work, but she hoped it would anyway.

The Bakehouse Three paused outside Happily Ever After to take in the window display. "Oh, I like that bronze satin," Carol said. The gown she was talking about had an off-the-shoulder neckline, long sleeves, and a full, mid-calf skirt. She put a hand to her chest. "I'd feel like a queen in that."

"And you'll look like one," Laura said, holding the door open for her friends.

Bells chimed as Molly stepped into the shop, which was warm and cozy. The aroma of lavender and roses drifted through the air. The whole effect made her think of a garden, bursting with pretty fabrics and colors.

A sales clerk with glossy black hair stepped forward. "Good afternoon," she said. "I'm Monica. How may I help you?"

Carol took the lead. "We're here to buy dresses for the Valentine's Day dinner and dance at Castleglen. I would love to try on the bronze satin in the window, if you have my size."

Monica's eyes deftly scanned Carol's figure. "Great choice. And I believe we do."

"We'll be browsing," Laura said.

While Carol followed the clerk toward the dressing rooms at the rear, Molly and Laura perused the racks. "So many choices," Laura said. "How will I narrow it down?"

Molly studied her friend's coloring. "Try green or violet dresses. They'll be beautiful with your auburn hair and brown eyes."

The dresses were organized by color, so Laura easily found a selection. Molly started toward the blue dresses—a favorite color because of her eyes—but then she stopped herself. Why not break out of the box a little this time?

A slim white dress with a round neckline called out to her. The bodice had an embroidered silver overlay that made her think of frost flowers. It had short sleeves but there was a matching bolero jacket in embroidered silver.

"Oh, Molly." Laura appeared at her side, holding several dresses on hangers. "That's gorgeous."

Molly fingered the silky skirt. "Isn't it? I'd need new shoes though. Silver or white to match this."

Laura whirled around and pointed. "And they have them. I'd go with silver."

Molly didn't have much use for silver shoes as a baker, so it would be a splurge. But how often did she splurge? Molly honestly couldn't remember the last time. She selected her size from the rack. "I'll try it on, then make a decision."

Carol was already behind the dark-pink velvet curtain of a changing room. Monica hovered nearby and opened the curtains on two stalls when she saw Laura and Molly coming. "Here you are, ladies. Let me know if you need any help."

"We will," Molly said, slipping inside a room with her one dress. If this didn't work, she'd probably fall back on something blue.

Laura disappeared into her changing room, drawing the curtain with a clatter of the rings. "How are you doing, Carol?" she called.

"Fine," Carol said. "I'm coming out in a minute. And I definitely want your opinion."

Molly was still working on removing her many winter layers when Carol announced that she was ready. Both Molly and Laura poked their heads out around their curtains. Carol stood in front of the triple mirror, moving side to side to study the gown.

Molly sucked in a breath. "You are stunning, Carol. Absolutely beautiful."

A shy smile crept over Carol's face. "You think so?" She patted her hair. "I'll have to figure out what to do with this mop."

"We'll go to the salon and get the full treatment," Molly said. "Hair and nails, even facials."

"I could use a facial," Laura said, patting her cheek. "Winter skin. And yes, Carol, that dress is perfect." She disappeared behind the curtain.

Molly closed her curtain too and finished changing into the gown. It fit perfectly, skimming over her midsection and flowing nicely around her legs.

She stepped out into the main room and took her place in front of the mirror. "I'm ready," she called to her friends. She saw in the mirror that Monica was talking to a new customer—Robina McDonald. With a jolt, Molly remembered her earlier conversation with Cole. Was this a good time to talk to Robina? Molly resolved that she'd at least try.

As Molly examined herself from different angles, she noticed Carol and Laura peering around their curtains at her. She swiveled in front of the mirror, the same way Carol had. "What do you think?"

"I love it," Carol said. "You could be a winter princess."

Molly giggled. "I'll take that description."

"Fergus will fall madly in love," Laura said, then snapped her fingers. "Oh, that's right. He already has."

"I hope so." A pang of insecurity struck Molly. He'd been so strange lately, almost blowing hot and cold.

"Hope so?" Carol snorted. "No doubt about it." She studied Molly's dress again. "You should get it."

Molly gazed into the mirror, deciding she agreed with Carol. Even with her hair full of static from her hat and not much makeup, she did look good. The dress was extremely flattering and the color worked on her.

"I second that," Laura said. She stepped out of her own changing room, a vision in violet velvet. The soft yet deep shade brought out the richness of her hair, the depth of her eyes. The long-sleeved dress was fitted at Laura's trim waist before cascading to the floor. Her knee peeked out of a tasteful slit on one side.

"Talk about royalty," Molly said. "Wow."

"Yes, wow is right," Carol said. "It's perfect."

Laura dipped her head in thanks. "I love it." She rubbed a hand across the fabric. "It's so soft and cozy."

Molly heaved a sigh. "I'm glad we all found something. I was not feeling a road trip right now."

"We're too busy for a road trip," Laura said. "And in this weather? No thanks."

Carol had gone behind the curtain again, but now she popped back out. "Oh, I've been meaning to ask you two. It's short notice but do you want to come over for dinner tonight? Harvey has a billiards date with Fergus and Trent."

"That would be fun," Molly said. "Let me know what to bring."

"Me too," Laura said. "I was just wondering what to eat tonight."

"We'll talk about it after we change," Carol said.

While Molly was putting her street clothes back on, she heard Monica and Robina chatting. Robina took the booth next to hers. By the time Molly emerged, Robina was standing in front of the mirror, dressed in a dove-gray skirt suit.

"That is super chic on you," Molly said.

"Think so?" Robina examined herself in the mirror. "It's for an upcoming interview on Geraldine Hughley's talk show."

Carol and Laura emerged with their new gowns and stopped to listen.

Recognizing the famous talk show host's name, Molly was impressed.

"An interview about your new show?" she asked. "Congratulations by the way." Although Robina was a strong suspect, she wasn't proven guilty yet, so polite congratulations were in order.

Robina nodded thanks. "It's been a long time coming," she said. "I got the idea ages ago, and everything finally came together."

"We're happy for you," Carol said. "Will you be featuring chocolates?"

The young woman's nose wrinkled. "I'm not picking up where Devon left off, if that's what you're asking. I want to do candy traditions around the world, with adapted recipes for the home cook. Plus my own original recipes."

"Sounds fun," Laura said. "I love making up my own recipes."

"Me too." Robina frowned. "And at least now I won't have someone else taking credit for my work."

Molly guessed who she was referring to but wanted to verify anyway. "Did Devon do that to you?" she asked sympathetically. "It must have been maddening."

Robina tugged at the hem of her jacket. "All the time. It can be a scramble producing a show, with not much time for prep work. So when he started asking me to take his ideas and create recipes, I was flattered. I thought it would eventually help me get ahead, that he might even feature me on an episode." Her laugh was bitter. "Even make me a cohost since I was doing more than half the work."

"But he didn't want that," Molly said.

"Nope." Robina lifted her chin, tears of anger glittering in her eyes. "It was always all about Devon. He was the star."

And apparently he didn't care who he trampled to get there. Molly thought of one more question. "Are you going to feature Superior Bay College in an episode? I understand you went there."

Color flamed in Robina's cheeks. "So what if I did? I graduated from a certain culinary institute in Vermont." She tossed her head, likely assuming they knew which school she was referring to. "That's the credential that counts."

"If it's the one I think you mean, it's a great school," Laura said. "I've worked with many graduates, and they are all top-notch."

The compliment appeared to mollify Robina. "Yes, they are. *We* are." She pivoted back to the mirror and studied her reflection, signaling that the conversation was over.

Molly got the hint. "See you later. Oh, and buy that."

"Maybe I will," Robina said in a musing tone.

Molly caught the sharp gleam in the driven young woman's eye reflected in the mirror and wondered exactly what lengths she'd go to in order to succeed.

15

Carol had decided to pull a homemade lasagna out of the freezer, so Molly made a tossed salad. Laura was doing garlic bread, also homemade.

Toting a big plastic bowl with lid, Molly guided Angus from the bakehouse out to the Honda. The night air was frosty and cold, the stars above on full display. There weren't any events at the Winter Faire this evening, so all was quiet over at the park. Lights still shone on the half-finished sculptures, though, making Molly shiver as they drove past. After what had happened to Devon, no one had the heart to keep going with that aspect of the faire. Everything else was still on, though, including Fergus's iceboat race tomorrow.

Picturing his boat whizzing across the ice at high speeds, Molly hoped it wouldn't be too exciting. Didn't people get hurt doing that?

Carol and Harvey lived about ten minutes out of town, in a log home right on the loch. Outside downtown, houses quickly became scattered, and streetlights were few and far between. Molly was alone on the road, which was glazed with a thin layer of snow and ice. Although she knew the road well, she proceeded with caution, taking the corners slowly and well under control.

She was on a straightaway with a short passing lane when headlights came into view behind her. Although she had seen very few cars on the road tonight, she didn't really pay attention to it.

Until the larger vehicle sped up with a roar and bright lights glared menacingly in her rearview mirror.

"Seriously?" Molly muttered to herself, causing Angus's ears to perk up in alarm. "You'll never make it." The straightaway was short and after it ended, there was no place to pass for a couple of miles.

Molly slowed to let the vehicle by, but he stayed behind her. After the passing lane ended, they entered a series of curves, marked by yellow warning signs.

The tailgater was inches from her bumper now, a large shadow copying her every move as she guided the Honda. Molly's hands broke into a sweat inside her gloves and tension tightened her shoulders. Sensing his owner's distress, Angus was now on high alert, issuing gruff woofs.

A sign indicated the worst corner of all, best taken at a crawl. Going off the road here meant flying into the woods. The Honda's tires slid on ice and Molly gasped. This section of road was often extra slippery due to the overhanging trees.

"Hang on, hang on," she told herself. "You've done this a million times."

Trying to focus on her driving instead of the vehicle looming behind her, Molly navigated out of the curve. Now the road opened up and was relatively free of snow and ice from what she could see.

Instinctively she hit the gas, but the other vehicle did too. Before Molly could figure out what to do, it swerved out into the other lane and blasted past her. She had time to notice that it was a pickup truck before it was gone, red taillights vanishing into the night.

She finally found Carol's driveway and parked beside Laura's Volkswagen Beetle with relief. As she and Angus got out, she glanced back toward the road. All was quiet again, not a single vehicle in sight.

It figured that she would see the only other person on the road tonight. Everyone with sense was tucked up in a warm house.

Her footsteps stuttered and Angus looked up at her in concern. What if the pickup had been following her? Or even trying to scare her?

Logically, Molly knew she was safe but that didn't stop her from running the rest of the way to the house. She knocked as she opened the door, the friends' usual ritual when they were expecting each other. "Hello?" she called. "I'm here."

"We're in the kitchen," Carol replied. The kitchen was on the other side of the spacious main room, where a fire crackled merrily in the stone fireplace.

Molly set her bowl down, unleashed Angus, and removed her gloves, coat, and boots while he scampered across the floor to greet Carol and Laura. She picked up the salad bowl and padded in her socks to join the others.

Laura was leaning on the island counter while Carol checked the oven. "Almost ready," Carol said. "Want to hand me the garlic bread?"

"Sure." Laura picked up a foil-wrapped log and brought it to Carol, Angus bouncing along at her heels. "Hey, Angus. Nice to see you."

Molly set the salad container on the island. "Guess what? I think someone followed me out here. They were tailgating me, especially on those sharp curves."

"People do that all the time," Carol said. "Out here in the country, they think speed limits don't apply."

"You could be right," Molly said hesitantly. "But whoever it was, he gave me a creepy feeling."

Laura returned from the refrigerator with a few bottles of salad dressing. "That worries me," she said with a frown. "You need to listen to your instincts, especially after last night."

"My instincts might be off on this one," Molly said. "I've been tailgated numerous times, so I could be overreacting." Her mind flashed back to the looming headlights, and fresh chills hit her. "But this felt menacing. What if it was the same person who grabbed me last night?" What if he was lurking, waiting for another chance to accost her?

"I sure hope not," Carol said, now sounding more concerned. "Harvey should follow you home. He ought to be back before you leave."

"Good idea," Laura said. "I'll feel better if he does."

"In that case, I'll definitely let him escort me." Molly decided it was time for a change of subject. She peeled the lid from the plastic bowl. "Where can I find salad servers?"

During dinner, they focused on the meal, keeping the topics of discussion light. More than once, someone remarked on how excited they were for the Valentine's Day dinner and dance.

"I didn't even let Harvey see my dress," Carol said with a chuckle. "I hid it in the spare room closet."

"You'll knock his socks off for sure," Laura said. "It'll be fun going on a formal date with Trent. It's probably time he found out what I look like in something other than hiking boots or a chef's coat."

Carol laughed. "I almost feel like we're headed to prom."

"Same here," Molly said. "Once you're out of school, there are so few opportunities to get all dolled up. It's a shame, really."

"There's not much outside the rare formal dance and occasional wedding," Carol said. "And a lot of weddings are casual now. I saw photos of a bride taking vows in shorts last summer, complete with veil and bouquet."

"That's a little too casual, even for me," said Laura, who usually avoided dresses. "But to each their own."

After dinner, they helped Carol clean up and load the dishwasher before adjourning to the living room, where they sprawled on the comfortable sofa and chairs to relax, sipping hot drinks.

"I have cookies," Carol said from the depths of the sofa. "Say the word and I'll go get them."

"I couldn't eat another bite," Molly said. "Honestly. What a great meal." The lasagna had been thick and cheesy, studded with chunks of spicy sausage. Laura's garlic bread was divine, fluffy and buttery with a crunchy crust. Molly's salad had been a light, refreshing complement, although vegetables in the winter weren't anywhere near as good as fresh local offerings in the other seasons.

Laura groaned in agreement. She was lying back, her neck resting on cushions and one hand idly scratching Angus, who was clearly enjoying the extra attention.

Molly thought about bringing up what was weighing on her mind, namely the two murder cases. But she was so warm and cozy right now, so content, that she decided to shelve it for the night. The next morning would be soon enough to pick it all up again.

"Tomorrow is the iceboat race," she said instead. "I hope Fergus does well." *And stays safe.*

Her phone beeped with a text. Thinking it might be Chloe, she reached out a lazy hand and picked it up. It was from Fergus. But wasn't he playing billiards at the resort with Harvey and Trent?

"Excuse me," Molly said, pressing the icon to open the message. She gasped. "Oh no. Why is he asking me that? What should I do?"

"What's the question?" Carol asked drowsily.

"Neil came down with the flu tonight, so Fergus wants me to race with him." Molly sat up straight, petrified. "On the iceboat."

"I vote yes," Laura said. "They're super fun. Fergus will take good care of you." She patted Angus. "Right, boy? Plus, you'll be dressed appropriately and wearing a helmet."

"That's comforting, I suppose," Molly said. But even skiers wore helmets nowadays. Should she do it or not? She stared into the flickering flames as if they held an answer.

"Ask yourself this," Carol said. "If you don't go, will you regret it? In life, it's often not the things we do that we regret, but whatever we weren't brave enough to try."

"When you put it like that..." Molly set her shoulders decidedly. "All right, I'll do it." Before she could change her mind, she texted back an affirmative.

His response was immediate and excited. *You're going to love iceboating,* he said. She sure hoped so.

Molly arrived at the iceboat race around nine the following morning. Other racers and spectators were tromping around, sipping from steaming mugs of coffee and chattering in excitement.

The iceboats were lined up on the frozen loch. To Molly's eyes, they resembled extra-long kayaks with masts. Metal runners underneath and out to each side would carry the craft along. She headed toward Fergus's iceboat, which was bright blue with white stripes, where he was raising the mast.

As she drew closer, she saw that some boats, like Fergus's, held two people seated side-by-side while others sat only one. For her first time racing or even stepping foot in an iceboat, she was glad to have a partner. To her surprise, she saw Cole Keith, the cameraman, and for once he wasn't behind the lens. He clearly intended to sail today. His one-man boat was bright red with a red-striped white sail.

Now busy working on the rigging, Fergus greeted her with a smile. "Morning, Molly. Your gear is right there." He nodded toward a duffel with a helmet sitting on top. "There are changing rooms by the sign-in desk."

Molly picked up the bag and helmet. "I'll be right back. Where should I leave this when I'm done?"

"By the sign-in area is fine. The bag has a tag with my name on it."

"Okay." She hesitated before heading off.

"Are you okay with this?" he asked. "I won't be upset if you don't want to go."

"No, I'll do it," Molly said, forcing herself into action. If she didn't race, he'd probably have to drop out. Even if he switched to the one-person race, his two-seater boat would never compete against the lighter singles.

A huge smile creased his handsome features. "Great. See you back here in a few."

Molly trudged over to the changing rooms, where she slipped inside and unzipped the duffel. Inside were special socks, short booties, and a neoprene suit with long arms and legs. The suit was surprisingly warm, so she stuffed her parka into the duffel along with her snow boots. A balaclava went over her head, hiding everything but her face.

Feeling like a character in an underwater epic, she stepped out of the changing room, duffel in one hand and helmet with goggles under her arm. She'd put that on at the iceboat.

"Molly," Laura called from the path leading to the parking lot. Carol was right behind her. "You look amazing."

"I guess that's one word for it," Molly said. "I'm surprisingly warm right now."

Laura touched the material. "That's a good suit. Trent sells these."

"I'm so glad you two are here," Molly said, touched that her friends had come to watch. "Bridget and Hamish holding down the fort?"

"They are indeed," Carol said. She patted her pocket. "I've promised to take video of the race for them."

Molly hefted the duffel. "I need to drop this off, if you want to walk with me."

They came along, and she placed the bag in a pile with others at the attendant's instruction.

"And now I'd better get going," Molly said. "Fergus's boat is the blue one with white stripes." She pointed it out. "We're in the two-person class." They called well wishes as she made her way back to Fergus.

He now had the sails attached to the mast. "I see the suit fits," he said after giving her a once-over. "I hoped I had the right size."

"It's perfect," Molly said. "A bit of a struggle getting it on, but it's really comfortable." She placed the helmet on her head and fastened the strap, then slid the goggles over her eyes. "I'm ready." Her belly flipped over. She hoped she was ready.

Soon they were lined up with the other iceboats in their class. "I'm going to push us off and hop in," Fergus said to Molly, who held the line controlling one of the sails. "You tug on that line when I give you the signal."

"Will do." Molly was squeezed into the narrow seat, finding it hard to believe that Fergus could fit in beside her. They would be very friendly, as her mother would say.

The gun went off, and Fergus began to push, his feet in cleats that gripped the ice. Then he hopped in with a "Go!" and Molly tugged on the line. The sail immediately filled with air and pulled them faster and faster across the ice.

The cold air rushing into her face stole Molly's breath. This was incredible. She felt like thistledown flying through the air. Only the scrape of the blades and Fergus's warm bulk kept her grounded.

"Like it?" he shouted, taking the line and adjusting the sail.

"Love it," she shouted back.

They were halfway across the loch when she noticed another iceboat coming in their direction, toward them instead of parallel like the other racers. "Fergus," she said, tugging on his arm.

He studied the oncoming iceboat. "What's he doing? That's a single. He's not supposed to be out here."

A red single. Cole had a red one-man, and his sail was white with a red stripe like this one. "That's Cole Keith, Devon's cameraman," Molly said. "He's racing today."

"Well, he's out of bounds right now." Fergus adjusted the sail to change their course. The other iceboat did the same, the lighter craft zipping closer every second. A collision seemed to be inevitable.

Molly realized the horrible truth. "He's trying to hit us!"

16

"Hang on!" Fergus shouted. As the other iceboat arrowed straight toward them, Fergus worked the tiller to change their course. At the same time, he instructed Molly on how to control the sail.

Couldn't the other sailor see them? Who would do such a thing? They could all be seriously injured—or worse. Molly hunched her shoulders and obeyed, wincing as she anticipated the crash and splintering of the iceboats when they hit.

All she could hear was the wind rushing in her ears and the scrape of the runners on the ice. They were in their own little bubble, the tension rising with every second.

Fergus adjusted the tiller again when the other iceboat was almost upon them.

Molly squeezed her eyes shut, not wanting to witness the crash.

"He missed us," Fergus said a moment later, relief in his voice. "Inches to spare."

Molly's eyes burst open, but her relief was short-lived. They were still shooting forward on the trajectory Fergus had set, headed straight for the shore of the loch—right toward a thick stand of trees.

"Let go of the line," Fergus called to Molly.

What would happen now? She managed to uncurl her fingers, which had been holding the line so tight they ached. The sail flapped harmlessly, and as if by magic, the iceboat slowed.

Fergus was able to correct their course enough that they ended up close to shore but parallel to the woods, rather than headed toward them.

Molly lay back, arms limp at her side. "We're not dead."

"No, we're not." Fergus cracked a wan smile. He rubbed a hand over his face. "That was a bit too exciting for me."

"I was bracing for impact, as they say." Molly sat up, noticing that people were running along the shore toward them. A couple of other iceboats were also zooming in their direction, having abandoned the race. "Here comes the cavalry." Wondering where the other iceboat had gone, she studied the loch.

"There he goes," Fergus said.

The red iceboat had stopped on the other shore. A small figure got out and raced into the woods. Several other iceboats were heading in that direction, probably hoping to track down the sailor.

"That tells me one thing for sure," Fergus said angrily. "He did it on purpose. Otherwise, why run away?"

The cold sinking into Molly's core told her he was right. "Cole Keith must be guilty," she blurted.

"Cole?" Fergus levered himself out of the iceboat, extending a hand to help Molly.

"That was Cole's boat," Molly said as she eased out of her seat. Her legs were wobbly from shock. "I saw him standing near it before the race. There are no other red iceboats here today."

Fergus put a hand to his brow to scan the loch. "You're right. He had a single boat?"

"Yes," Molly said. "Same as the one that came at us."

"Are you two all right?" Officer Murdoch wheezed. He leaned over and braced his hands on his thighs. "I got here as fast as I could."

Carol, Laura, and other onlookers crowded behind him, most of them huffing and puffing too.

"I'm glad you're not picking us up out of the woods," Fergus said, his voice grim. "Or scraping us off the ice."

Carol and Laura trotted over to hug Molly. "Are you okay?" Carol asked. "We saw the whole thing."

"I was so scared," Laura said. "I thought for sure the two iceboats were going to crash."

"I'm okay—now," Molly said. "Fergus did a masterful job of piloting."

"He really did," Carol said. "It was amazing."

Fergus pointed to the red iceboat on the shore. "Officer Murdoch, Molly says Cole Keith owns that boat. We saw him run into the woods. Maybe someone can intercept him over there, on that side."

The pursuing iceboats, now stopped near Cole's craft, seemed to have had the same idea. A couple of people had gotten out to follow Cole into the woods, but were hampered by the deep snow and thick trees.

Officer Murdoch squinted at the shoreline. "I'll send a cruiser over. I'm guessing he'll come out on the road near Superior Bay College." He spoke into his chest radio, giving directions.

"Cole did it on purpose," Molly told Officer Murdoch once he finished his message. "He deliberately came right at us. Plus, he shouldn't even have been out on the ice yet. He was in a single and they weren't in this race." Why had Cole done it? To scare her off? Had he been driving the pickup the night before? Had he grabbed her outside the changing hut? He had tried to implicate Robina, she recalled. Was that to throw Molly off the scent?

"She's right," Laura said. "We saw it happen." Other people in the crowd called out agreement.

"I don't like the sound of this," Officer Murdoch said. "Someone accosted you the other night, Molly." He cocked a brow. "Sounds to me like it might be related."

Molly shivered. "I was thinking the same thing."

"I'm on it," Murdoch said. "I assure you we'll catch up with him sooner or later. If it was deliberate, charges will be filed."

"Thank you, Officer," Molly said. "I appreciate it."

"What's going on with the race now?" Fergus asked. "They're supposed to have the singles race next."

"They halted the racing for now," Officer Murdoch said. "They'll go again in an hour."

"I'm going to sail the iceboat back to the landing," Fergus told Molly. "Do you want to come with me?"

Molly considered his offer. Right now, she never wanted to get into an iceboat again. In fact, at the thought, her legs felt rooted to the spot. But how could she let him go alone? What if something else happened and she was stuck on shore, unable to help him?

"I'll go," she said. "I'm your first mate, and first mates don't quit."

His lips curved in a smile. "No, they don't." He rested a hand on her shoulder. "You're the best, Molly."

"See you back at the landing," Officer Murdoch said. "I'll take your full statement then."

Molly waved goodbye to Carol and Laura, then followed Fergus back onto the ice. She helped him position the iceboat in the right direction before climbing in. Once more, he pushed off and then leaped inside. She handled the sail and he worked the tiller, and soon they were back at the starting line.

She climbed out and helped him scoot the iceboat onto the shore. Her stomach rumbled. "As soon as we're done here, I'm getting something to eat." With all the excitement, her breakfast was long gone.

"Molly," Fergus said, his tone urgent. When she looked up at him, she noticed how serious his expression had become. "I want you to stay at the resort tonight. Until this situation is resolved, I don't want you being alone."

She was touched by his obvious concern. And come to think of it, she didn't want to be alone in her apartment either, although Angus was a great guard dog—or at least he thought he was. "Do you have room for me? You said you were full."

"There's always room for you, Molly." Fergus let go of the iceboat and reached into his pocket for his phone. "I'll make a call right now."

Molly warmed to the idea. She'd bring Angus, and she could order room service tonight. Maybe she'd even pop into the resort spa for a facial. After the last few days, she could use a treat like that.

Carol and Laura found them. "I have the perfect idea for lunch," Carol said. "One of the food trucks has corn chowder."

"I love corn chowder," Molly said. She tugged at her neoprene sleeve. "Let me go get changed, and I'll be right with you."

She retrieved her bag from the sign-in area and trudged off to the changing room. The door to the cubicle she'd used before was ajar, but when she pushed on it, it wouldn't budge. How strange. Had the wedge used to hold it open gotten caught?

A man was walking past.

"Excuse me," Molly said. "Can you help me a second? The door is stuck."

"Sure." After checking the gap underneath, the man put his shoulder to the door and pushed hard. "There's something blocking it." He moved closer and peered around the door. "There's a man lying on the floor. I wonder if he had a heart attack or something."

Was the man ill? Or worse? Molly staggered back a couple of steps, dropping her duffel. "I'll go get help."

"I think it's one of the racers," the man reported. "He's wearing a neoprene suit."

Molly ran back to the sign-in area, hoping to find someone to help. Officer Murdoch was talking to the attendant, going over something on the table. "Officer Murdoch," she called.

"I'll be with you in a few," Officer Murdoch said. "Stick around, okay?"

"I'm not here about my statement," Molly said. "A man is sick or something inside a changing room. He fell on the floor and he's blocking the door."

Officer Murdoch leaped into action. An ambulance was on standby, so he called the EMTs over. He rounded up some other helpers, including Fergus, and soon they had the door off so they could reach the stricken man.

Molly couldn't hold back a gasp when his face was revealed.

Cole Keith.

"How is this possible?" Molly's gaze sought out Fergus. "He chased us in the iceboat and ran onto the other shore." There hadn't been time for him to come back to the park and end up in the changing room, nor could he have done it unobserved.

The EMTs were checking Cole over, and after a minute, one helped him sit up. "Someone hit him on the head," one medic said. "But he's conscious now. Vitals are good."

Molly exhaled a breath. What a relief. For a few minutes there, she'd thought she had stumbled across another murder victim.

"Who did this to you?" Officer Murdoch asked, leaning close.

Cole blinked, one hand going to the back of his head. "I don't know." He glanced around in confusion, wincing. "I came in here to put on another layer. I don't remember anything beyond that."

Molly frowned. "Whoever hit you must have stolen your iceboat."

Cole's eyes widened. "My iceboat? Where is it?" He struggled to get up. "I hope it's not damaged. It's a rental."

"It's fine," Officer Murdoch said. "Parked on the other side of the loch, but fine."

"We need to take him to the medical center to get checked out," an EMT said. "He might have a concussion."

Officer Murdoch backed up. "All right, everyone. Clear the area.

Let them do their job." He nodded at Cole. "I'll come by the hospital to take a full statement later."

"We'll get someone to retrieve your iceboat," Fergus told Cole. "You concentrate on healing."

Molly decided she'd change at home. Retrieving her bag, she followed Fergus back around the building. "Someone hit him and stole the iceboat."

"Looks that way," Fergus said. He scanned the loch, where the other sailors had abandoned pursuit of the renegade iceboater and were returning to the starting area. "I hope the police catch up with him or her." A moment later, he gave a sigh of relief. "Oh, good. They're towing the other iceboat back. That's one item we can check off."

Carol and Laura were talking to Hamish's wife, Joyce. Seeing Molly and Fergus, they excused themselves. "What's going on?" Carol asked. "You're still in your iceboating gear."

"We found Cole unconscious in a changing room," Molly said. She waved at Joyce, whom she adored. "He wasn't piloting the iceboat that almost hit us."

"Someone bashed him on the head and stole it," Fergus put in. "And so far, it seems whoever it was got away."

"I guess that eliminates Cole as a suspect," Laura said. "At least in this instance."

"This case is so frustrating," Molly said. "Everything points in one direction and then bam! It shifts to another."

"See you at the resort later?" Fergus asked Molly. "Let me know when you check in." He gave her a quick hug. "And now I'd better run. I need to dismantle my iceboat and get back to the resort."

"Oh, Fergus," Molly said, realizing what this meant for him. "What a disappointment. You didn't get to finish your race."

"There will be other races," Fergus said. "What matters to me is that you weren't hurt."

Carol, who didn't miss a trick, said, "Are you staying at the resort tonight, Molly? Good idea."

"I asked her to, until this situation is cleared up," Fergus said. "I want her somewhere I can keep an eye on her." He winked.

Molly took the opportunity to lighten the mood. "Face it—I'm a magnet for trouble."

He wrapped his arms around her again. "And a very pretty one too."

"You're not so bad yourself," Molly said, ignoring Carol and Laura's teasing.

He kissed her gently. "See you soon."

After a bowl of corn chowder at the faire, Molly relieved Hamish at the bakehouse. Once they closed, she went up to the apartment to pack an overnight bag. If she needed to stay another night, she'd grab more clothes when she worked the next day.

"We're in for a treat," she told Angus, who was anxiously watching her. Whenever she pulled out suitcases, he went on high alert. He knew that meant his person was going somewhere and might be leaving him behind. "You're coming with me this time, mister."

He bounced on all four paws, excited. Then he dashed out of the bedroom and came back a moment later with his favorite toy in his mouth. He dropped the stuffed sheep onto the carpet, then gazed at her expectantly, wagging his tail.

Molly laughed. "You want me to pack Woolie? Not a problem." She scooped it off the floor and tossed it into her suitcase.

Angus plopped down, now content to supervise. After finishing with her own packing, Molly gathered dog food and treats, then strapped a tartan coat on him. He was so jaunty in his Scottish attire.

Although there wasn't a set time to check in, Molly wanted to get to the resort before dark. Her encounter with the mysterious pickup had shaken her, especially in light of the events at the iceboat race. There was no doubt that someone was targeting her, trying to throw her off track.

As she drove the familiar route, she wondered if Chief Thomson was fully aware of recent events. She decided to give him a call, using her car's hands-free feature.

She got through immediately. "Molly," Chief Thomson said. "I heard about the incident at the race today. Are you okay?"

"I'm fine, Chief. But I'm heading over to the resort to spend the night. Fergus insisted."

"So he believes that the near-crash wasn't an accident?"

"It definitely wasn't, Chief," Molly said. She knew from long experience that the chief was cautious about jumping to conclusions. It was part of what made him so good at his job. "The one-man iceboats weren't even racing yet. And he came right at us." Molly slowed as she neared the resort entrance. "Plus, the iceboat was stolen from Cole Keith."

"Yes, that's a very good point. And in that gear they wear, well, you might not even recognize your own grandmother."

"That's right. We couldn't see his or her face. With the helmet and goggles, it could have been anyone." She paused before adding, "Except Carol, who was on shore the whole time." Molly wasn't going to miss the opportunity to issue a gentle rebuke of the suspicions the police and prosecutor had regarding her friend.

"Noted," the chief said.

"I also had a truck follow me in a rather threatening way the other night. I don't know how else to describe it. I wouldn't mention it at all, but given everything else that's going on, I figured I'd better."

"I'm glad you did. Tell me what happened."

"It wasn't too bad, but it scared me. And it might have been nothing more than an impatient or especially bad driver." With that disclaimer, she described the incident.

"I don't suppose you got the license plate," the chief said when she was finished.

"No such luck," Molly said. "I didn't get a good look at it." She pulled through the stone pillars into the resort parking lot, slowing to scope out a space. "I'm at the resort now, Chief, so I'd better let you go. Thanks for the chat."

"No problem, Molly," the chief said. "Please keep me posted if anything else strange or out of place happens."

"I'll do that." Molly slid into a spot and shut off the engine. "Have a good night."

Molly gathered her bags and leashed Angus, then strode at top speed toward the main entrance, eager to get out of the blustery wind.

The entrance doors opened with a gentle whoosh, and she stepped into the warm and elegant lobby with a sigh of gratitude. The desk attendant greeted her with a smile, and across the room, a fire blazed in a huge stone fireplace. People lounged in comfortable furniture around the room with hot beverages, chatting quietly and relaxing before they headed to their rooms or to dinner.

A woman with an uneven gait was approaching the desk from the other direction, and Molly politely hung back to let her handle her business first. Then she realized who it was.

Robina McDonald, and she was limping, which was new. She'd been fine when Molly ran into her at Happily Ever After. Had Robina been injured recently?

Perhaps while piloting a rogue iceboat?

M olly hung back while Robina took care of her business with the front desk, not wanting to eavesdrop. As she waited, images from the disastrous iceboat race raced through her mind: The unidentifiable figure in the other craft steering directly toward her and Fergus. Missing them and landing on the other shore. Leaping out and dashing into the woods.

At that distance, it had been difficult to gauge the person's size and weight. Everyone looked the same in the neoprene suits too, like sleek seals on two legs. It was very possible that Robina was responsible. Maybe she'd slipped or tripped in the forest while running away and twisted a knee or ankle.

Should Molly talk to Robina? Her injury gave her the perfect excuse to question her, about that at least. As the other woman finished her conversation and started away from the desk, Molly was torn. If she checked in now, Robina would probably disappear, back to her room or somewhere else in the resort.

But then Robina hesitated and faced the attendant again. "One more thing. Can someone please bring me a mug of hot chocolate? I'd like to sit by the fire for a while."

"Certainly, Ms. McDonald," the clerk said, picking up the phone. "Have a seat and it will be right out."

"Thank you." Robina limped away and selected a love seat near the fire.

Assured that Robina wouldn't be leaving just yet, Molly went up to the desk after the clerk hung up. "Hi, I'm Molly Ferris. I have a room booked for tonight."

"Of course, Mrs. Ferris." The clerk smiled knowingly. "You're Mr. MacGregor's guest."

"That's right," Molly said, proud to claim such a distinction.

"Make that guests." The clerk smiled over the counter at Angus. "What a cutie." Angus wagged his tail at the compliment, and Molly was pleased that Fergus had included Angus in the reservation. The resort didn't typically allow pets, but well-behaved Angus had been an exception before and would be again today.

"He's a good boy," Molly said. "And very excited about his stay at the resort."

After some typing and mouse clicking, the clerk handed Molly a room key. "The Wi-Fi password is on the envelope," she said. "Room service menus are in the room. And if there is anything you need, anything at all, please don't hesitate to call down."

"Thank you," Molly said.

"Have a good night," the clerk said with a smile.

Key envelope in hand, Molly gathered her bags and made a beeline for Robina, Angus trotting along behind. Robina had been served a mug of hot chocolate and rested with one leg stretched out beside her on the love seat, clearly content.

Molly almost felt guilty for interrupting her. Almost. "Hi, Robina," she said brightly.

Robina peered up at Molly, her gaze distant at first. Then her eyes cleared. "Oh, hi. I didn't expect to see you here." She glanced at Molly's luggage. "Don't you live in Loch Mallaig?"

"I do." Molly set her bags down and perched on an adjacent chair. "I didn't expect to be here tonight either, but I have an in with the owner and he invited me to stay. I'm definitely getting room service tonight."

"Yeah, it's a treat the first hundred times." Robina gave a world-weary sigh. "I was getting restless so I came down here for a change of scene. Don't get me wrong—our suite is gorgeous. I simply needed something different for a bit."

Our suite? "Oh, the suites are great here. Who are you sharing with?"

"Cole and Devon." Robina wrinkled her nose. "Well, it's me and Cole now. They finally cleaned out Devon's room, which is good. It was creepy before with all his clothes still in there and the bed unmade."

Molly could imagine. The police would have sealed off the room until they were done with it, and only then could it be cleared of Devon's possessions.

"How's Cole doing?" Molly asked. "Is he still at the hospital?"

"Yes, but they're going to release him." Not meeting Molly's eye, Robina smoothed the leg of her yoga pants. "He has to watch for a concussion, though."

"I'm so glad he's okay," Molly said. She almost told Robina that she'd found him but held back. "Such a strange thing to happen."

"It was," Robina said. "I missed the whole thing. I was here at the resort working on ideas for my show."

"I'm sure you have a lot of calls and video conferences right now," Molly said, hoping to tease out an alibi.

"I do, but I didn't have any today. For once I had enough free time to concentrate and do some research." Robina sat back and gave a small smile. "Research is nearly as fun as trying new recipes."

"We're the same way at the bakehouse," Molly said. Internally, she was wondering how she could bring up Robina's limp. "Always trying to come up with something different and yummy."

"You do a nice job." Robina's tone was slightly condescending. "Especially for a bakery in the middle of nowhere." She shook her head. "I never thought I'd come back here. In fact, I was shocked when Devon suggested it."

"Did you know him back when you were at Superior Bay together?" Molly asked.

"Not really," was the quick answer. "I mean I knew who he was. And the others too. They were students everyone admired. The golden gang, as it were." Her laugh was ironic. "Look at them now."

"I understand Marla was quite charismatic," Molly said. Dr. Pryde, for one, still seemed disconcerted by Marla's fall from grace.

"Oh, she was," Robina said. "We freshman girls used to talk about her all the time. We'd copy her outfits, gossip about her love life, and wish we were her."

"What did you think happened to her?"

Robina picked invisible lint from her pants. "We thought she killed herself. It was scary. If someone like that could crack under pressure—well, how could we handle it?" She jerked up her chin and leaned closer. "We thought it was Dr. Pryde's fault. Some students even tried to start a petition to get rid of him."

Molly frowned. What a nightmare for the professor. Yes, he was tough, but coddling students didn't do them any favors. He'd also believed that Marla had plagiarized her paper. But what if she hadn't? What if she'd come to him with accusations of unfair grading and teaching practices? Tenure or not, he wouldn't have welcomed the controversy.

Did Dr. Pryde kill Marla? Molly's mind shied away from that remote idea, but then she wondered if he'd had some reason to kill Devon. He was quite elderly now—which might explain why Devon was poisoned. It didn't take much strength to poison someone, merely knowledge and opportunity.

Just what I don't need—another suspect. With an effort, Molly reeled in her unruly thoughts. "That must have been quite an ordeal for Dr. Pryde," she said. "He's still there and he's still tough, according to Bridget, who is taking his class."

"I never had him," Robina said. "But that's not why I left Superior Bay. I realized I wanted more of a full culinary program and my school in Vermont offered that. Plus, it's such a great place."

"So I've heard." Molly rose to her feet. "I'd better get up to my room and settle in. It's almost Angus's dinnertime." She picked up her bags before casually saying, "I noticed you were limping. Did you hurt your leg?"

Robina glanced down at her outstretched leg. "Silly me. I slipped on the ice when I took a walk around the grounds. I wrenched my knee, but thankfully it's not too bad. I keep icing it."

Was she telling the truth? Molly couldn't tell. "You have to be careful around here in the winter. I've fallen down more than once. Hope your knee feels better soon."

Robina nodded dismissively, then shifted her attention to her phone. Molly led Angus toward the elevator and pushed the button for the fourth floor. When the doors opened, she followed the signs down the hall to her room.

Fergus had given her a suite, Molly realized when she entered. She had a plush sitting area with kitchenette and an attached bedroom, plus a luxurious bathroom with a rainwater shower and a soaking tub. Tall windows overlooked the loch, the curtains drawn against the cold night. A small fire flickered in the gas fireplace.

She unleashed Angus, who immediately ran to explore, and sent Fergus a text. *How sweet of you to give me a suite. It's lovely.*

You're welcome, he wrote back. *I'll pop up later when I can. Neil is a little better but still sick, so I'm handling some of his duties.*

Do what you need to do. Molly understood. Castleglen was quite the operation, and the buck stopped with Fergus.

An idea trickled into her mind and she fired off another text to Carol and Laura. *Want to join me for dinner and a movie in my suite at Castleglen?* This room was too nice to keep all to herself.

"They're going to come over," Molly told Angus when she got two enthusiastic answers. "And I'm taking a hot bubble bath before they get here."

After a long soak that steamed the chill out of her bones, Molly dressed in fleece lounging pants and a matching top. She was slipping thick socks onto her feet when someone knocked. "Coming," she called.

She peeked through the peephole, fully expecting to see Carol and Laura, who should be here any second. But it was Robina. Should she answer the door? What if Robina was the killer?

Curiosity won out.

"Robina," Molly said as she opened the door. "Please come in. I thought you were Carol and Laura. You know, my bakehouse partners. They'll be arriving within the next few minutes." If Robina was here for nefarious reasons, at least now she knew Molly was expecting company.

"Hope you don't mind, I saw your room number on your key envelope." The other woman winced as she limped into the room. "I won't be staying long." She made her way to one of the sofas and sat. "Cole is back from the hospital."

"How's he doing?" Molly remained standing, waiting for the next knock on the door.

"Pretty good." Angus came over to see Robina, and she stretched out her hand for him to sniff. "He has a headache, but otherwise he's okay." She gave the Scottie a scratch behind the ears.

"I'm glad to hear that," Molly said. "Now we need to figure out who hit him on the head, stole his iceboat, and almost crashed into Fergus and me." She watched Robina closely while she said this.

Robina continued to pat Angus, who was loving the attention. "I think I know who it was."

Molly took a step back. "Really? You should call the police and tell them."

When Robina looked down at Angus, Molly quickly switched on her phone's voice recorder.

"I'm not sure about calling the police," Robina said. "What if I'm wrong?"

"They can sort that out. But if you know something, you should go to them."

Robina stopped patting Angus and picked up a throw pillow instead, holding it to her midsection. "It's more a suspicion. Well, no. More than that. He has been acting really strange lately. I never knew why Devon kept letting him come around. He gives me the creeps."

There was only one person Robina could be referring to. "Are you talking about Blane Tully?"

Robina nodded. "I heard him fighting with Devon the day before he died. I was in my room when they came into the suite. I don't think they knew I was there. Blane started chewing Devon out, accusing him of stealing his family recipes."

"He said the same thing to me when I went to his shop to buy chocolates," Molly said. "He sounded really bitter about it."

"Do you blame him?" Robina huffed. "I wasn't surprised since Devon did the same thing to me, like I told you."

"Devon did have a bad habit of borrowing, it seems," Molly said. "From what my friend Laura has said, it happens all the time in the food industry."

"That doesn't make it right," Robina said. "And it's not borrowing, it's stealing."

Someone knocked on the door, and Molly practically flew over to see who it was. Carol and Laura were standing in the hallway. She hastily opened the door. "Please, come in. Robina stopped by to visit."

Carol raised a skeptical eyebrow, but she straightened her face when she walked in. "Hello, Robina. How are you?"

Molly's visitor twisted to face the newcomers. "I'm okay." She made a face as she put her hand on her leg. "Hurt my knee earlier." She pushed on the sofa arm and stood. "I'll get out of the way, Molly. But think about what I said, okay?"

"And I suggest you call Chief Thomson," Molly replied. "He'll be very interested to hear what you told me."

Carol and Laura didn't say anything until Robina was gone, the door clicking shut behind her.

"What did she tell you?" Carol asked.

"And how did she hurt her knee?" Laura frowned. "It wasn't while running through the woods after ditching an iceboat, was it?"

"I wondered that too." Molly stopped recording on her phone, then took their coats and hung them in a small closet. "As for what she said, it wasn't much. She overheard an argument between Devon and Blane about Blane's family recipes. He accused Devon of stealing them."

"Nothing new there," Carol said. "And I wonder why she decided to share that with you now."

"I know why," Laura said. "She's trying to cast blame on Blane. She doesn't want to go to the police because she's trying to stay under the radar."

"You're probably right," Molly said. "Which makes me very glad that you two showed up when you did. It was a dumb move to let her in."

"We'd have saved you if the going got rough," Carol said with a wink.

Molly chuckled, then went to a small table. "Moving on to more important things, like dinner." She opened a drawer and pulled out a room service menu. "Take a look and I'll place the order. And then we're going to forget about murders and iceboat crashes and bad guys for tonight, okay?"

She smiled at her friends, but her tone was firm. They all needed a break. Tomorrow was soon enough to pick up the investigation again. As for tonight, she was going to enjoy herself—then double-lock her door once Carol and Laura went home.

Bridget rushed to give Molly a hug when she walked into the bakehouse kitchen the next morning. "I heard about the iceboat race yesterday. Are you all right?"

Molly returned the hug. "I'm fine, but thank you for caring. I stayed at the resort last night and I'm so relaxed." She covered a big yawn with her hand. "See?" Even though she'd gotten an excellent night's sleep, Molly was still tired. The ordeal of the past week had taken a toll. Unfortunately, it wasn't over yet—not until Marla and Devon's killers had been arrested.

"Ooh, you got a manicure?" Bridget took Molly's hand and studied her freshly painted nails.

"We all did, after an excellent room service dinner," Carol piped up from where she was pouring cake batter into molds.

"It did me a world of good to be pampered for a bit," Laura added, punching down bread dough.

"Then we watched a movie and had popcorn and dessert." Molly reached for an apron. "How's school?"

Bridget's eyes glowed. "Great, now that my paper is done. Fingers crossed Dr. Pryde likes it. Next up, I need to focus on my chemistry labs. I got behind while working on the paper. It's not too bad, but I will need to buckle down for the next couple of days."

"I remember those days. There's always something in the queue," Molly said as she went to the sink to wash up. "Do you need to leave early?"

"Would you mind? I don't want to leave you in the lurch."

"Hamish is coming in at noon. Can you stay until eleven?"

"Perfect," Bridget said. "That will give me a couple of hours before another study group this afternoon."

Molly studied their young employee. Judging by the way Bridget's eyes shone, she was pleased about more than just school going well. "All right, spill young lady. What are you so happy about?"

Pink crept into Bridget's cheeks. "I-I don't know what you mean."

Laura snorted. "Nonsense."

Molly raised an eyebrow at her. "You're practically giddy."

"Okay, you got me. I should have known I couldn't hide it from you. Neil asked me to the Valentine's dance." Bridget gave a little squeal. "I'm so excited."

"That's wonderful, Bridget," Molly said, and she meant it. As she'd suspected, a romance had been blossoming before her eyes. "You'll have to sit with us."

Carol and Laura chimed in with exclamations of excitement.

"You can't do better than Neil," Carol declared.

"And the same is true for him," Laura added.

"We've been friends for a while, but recently something seems to have shifted." Bridget beamed at them. "Now it's like a dam has burst and I can't stop smiling."

"I hope he never stops making you smile," Molly said, a warm sensation coursing through her as she thought about how Fergus had the same effect on her.

She floated on that cloud for much of the morning. Business in the bakehouse was steady with events at the faire still underway. From the conversations Molly overheard, many people came in mainly to warm up. As long as they bought something to eat or drink, though, she didn't mind.

Molly was getting ready to take a lunch break when she saw Cole sitting alone at a table. He had his laptop open and was tapping away at the keyboard. She detoured over to his table. "How are you feeling, Cole?"

"I'm okay. Head still hurts." He paused his typing and put a hand to his head, which sported a white bandage. "I understand you found me yesterday."

"I did," Molly said. "After the iceboat race, I wanted to put on my regular clothes. You were in the changing room."

"Have a seat." Cole gestured to an empty chair beside him. "I can't thank you enough. Who knows how long I would have been lying there otherwise?"

Molly perched on the edge of the chair. "Someone else would have come along, I'm sure." But he was right. Since the races were underway, people wouldn't have been changing for at least another hour or two. It wouldn't have been good for him to lie unconscious in a barely heated space.

And what if the head injury had killed him? The similarities to Devon's demise and discovery chilled her. Cole might have become another mysterious death.

"Do you have any idea who hit you?" she asked, unable to resist the question.

He pressed his lips together and shook his head. "No. And I wish I did, believe me. It's so frustrating. I heard footsteps, but before I could turn around, they whacked me good."

"That's so scary. I'm sorry that happened to you." Molly glanced at his computer. "What are you working on? Editing videos?"

"Yep. I'm editing down my B-roll from the faire." His shoulders relaxed, and he flexed his fingers, clearly relieved at the change of subject.

Molly leaned closer, taking in a series of thumbnails lining the screen, which displayed scenes from the dogsled race, the snowmobile event, and the snowshoe race.

"Want to watch any in particular?" Cole asked.

"Do the snowshoe race," Molly said. "I was in that one." Maybe he'd caught her flopping around on snowshoes.

He ran the video, which showed the racers lining up and setting off, legs pumping and puffs of snow flying. When he zoomed in on the spectators, Molly recognized Dr. Dunbar. Beside her stood a man in an orange jacket.

Molly put up her hand. "Stop."

Though Cole appeared puzzled, he did as she said, freezing the view of the pair.

"Do you know who that is in the orange jacket standing beside Dr. Dunbar?" Molly asked.

His brows drew together in puzzlement. "That's Blane Tully. You know, the guy who owns the candy store."

18

Blane Tully. Had Blane grabbed her outside the changing room? The chocolate-scented glove made sense if so. Probably everything he wore picked up scent from his kitchen. Had he followed her to Carol's as well, again trying to scare her?

"What does Blane drive?" she asked.

"I have no idea," Cole said, wrinkling up his forehead. "Why?"

Molly merely shook her head. She wasn't going to discuss her theories with him. "Do you think Blane hit you in the changing room?"

He continued to frown. "I have no idea. And I don't get the connection between seeing him with Brianne and someone stealing my iceboat."

Molly didn't either, not completely. But she did remember that Dr. Dunbar and Blane had been arguing in the woods. Were they working together? She recalled the part she'd overheard.

"That's it. I'm done."

"I'll decide that."

That could have been Blane refusing to work with Dr. Dunbar any longer, rather than refusing to continue the snowshoe race, as she had assumed. But the attack outside the changing room, tailgating, and iceboat race had all occurred after that conversation. Or—what if the professor was blackmailing Blane about Devon's death? Or Marla's. Or both, even. He wanted to stop paying, but she wouldn't let him.

Molly gave a little yelp, causing Cole to regard her in concern.

"Are you okay? You have a strange expression on your face."

"I'm fine," Molly said, trying to smile. "I guess all of this is wearing on me, that's all."

"Wearing on you?" Cole snorted. "I'm the one who got bonked on the head. Good thing the iceboat wasn't damaged. I would have lost my deposit."

"I'm glad the iceboat was okay," Molly said. "And that it didn't impale me and Fergus. Those runners are pretty sharp, I understand."

Cole made a strangled sound then covered his mouth. "Oh my. It didn't really sink in until now. You two might have been killed, or at least seriously injured."

"Yes, we might have been," Molly said. "But Fergus is an expert sailor and he managed to evade the other iceboat." She decided to probe while he was still feeling some sympathy toward her. "Are Brianne and Blane close?"

"Not really." Cole clicked the keys again but kept glancing at her, signaling that he didn't mind talking. "Brianne couldn't stand Blane back when we were in college. He was a bit of a buffoon and rather crude at times."

Molly pictured the refined young woman turning up her nose at a cloddish acquaintance. "What about in later years? No one other than those two stayed in Loch Mallaig, right?" Perhaps living in the same small town had brought them closer, along with maturity on Blane's part.

"All I know is that she was doing the nutritional analysis on his candy for his labels. She wrote to Devon and offered her services to him as well." Cole shrugged. "But other than that, we never communicated much after college. It was only when Devon decided to come back that everyone reconnected."

"Why did he come back?" Molly asked.

"To be honest, I think he got the idea from another cable show,"

Cole said. "They did a homecoming segment, and he realized Loch Mallaig was perfect for a feature too, especially with the Winter Faire going on." His eyes grew sad. "None of us had any idea Marla's body would be discovered while we were here."

"It must have been an incredible shock," Molly said.

Cole put a hand to his chest. "I'll never get over it. I loved that girl with all my heart."

"I'm so sorry," Molly murmured. She rose to her feet. "I'll let you get back to work." She peeked into his empty mug. "Would you like a refill?"

"No, that's okay, thanks." Cole shut the laptop lid and began winding the cord. "I need to get going."

Molly wished him a good day, then left him to pack up his computer. She'd report on their conversation to Carol and Laura, then run upstairs to eat lunch and let Angus out. He'd been cooped up all morning.

She found Carol and Laura in the kitchen. "Did Bridget leave?" she asked.

"A few minutes ago," Laura said. In a rare moment of relaxation, she was sitting on a stool and nibbling on a scone while reading the local newspaper.

"What were you and Cole talking about?" Carol asked.

"Remember when I was in the snowshoe race?" Molly asked. "I overheard Dr. Dunbar and a man talking in the woods. Apparently it was Blane. Cole had filmed them together at the race and I recognized Blane's orange jacket."

"They do know each other," Carol reminded her. "It might have been totally innocent."

"You're right," Molly agreed. "But listen to this." She quoted the conversation she'd overheard. "I'm going to put it in the suspicious column for now."

Laura tipped her head back and forth, thinking. "Add that to what Robina said last night and it sounds like Blane was definitely angry with Devon." She pointed a finger. "Plus the chocolate gloves. Probably everything Blane wears smells like chocolate."

"Exactly what I was thinking. Still, nothing is definitive," Molly said. "Cole also mentioned that Dr. Dunbar did the nutritional analysis for Blane's labels."

Carol's mouth dropped open. "And Blane uses apricots."

"Yes I know," Molly said. "I told Chief Thomson about that. He has access to a source of cyanide."

"I'm not talking about Blane," Carol said, arching a brow. "Who among that whole group is a scientist? Quite a renowned one too, I understand."

"Dr. Dunbar," Molly said. "And since she was doing work for him, she probably went to his shop."

"But they didn't find anything in the school kitchens," Laura said. "I don't think."

Understanding dawned on Molly. Dr. Dunbar, knowing that the police might search the kitchens, must have used another facility at the college—such as the chemistry labs.

"But did they search the chemistry labs?" Molly asked, panic beginning to grow. "Bridget is working there this afternoon. I'd better warn her to be careful around Dr. Dunbar." She dug her phone out of her pocket and dialed Bridget, but it merely rang and rang. Molly sent a text but it went unanswered.

Maybe she was overreacting, but Molly would prefer to know for sure that Bridget was okay. She snatched her coat off the peg, slid it on, and found her gloves in the pockets. "Forget about lunch. I'm going out to the college to find Bridget." She was halfway out the door when she remembered Angus. "Can one of you please walk Angus for me?"

"No problem," Carol said. "I'll go right up. Keep us posted, okay?"

"Will do." Molly tugged on her hat as she raced to her car. Within moments she was on her way to Superior Bay College. Using her hands-free system, she tried Bridget again. Still no answer, and she hadn't responded to Molly's text either.

Breathing deeply, she reminded herself to calm down. Bridget was probably busy, deep in an experiment in the lab. There was something she could do while on the road, though.

Molly called the police station, and once again was fortunate to be patched right through to Chief Thomson. "Hi, Molly. How are you today?"

"I'm fine, Chief. I have some more updates for you."

After a pause, he said, "Go ahead. But I do have a meeting in five minutes."

"I'll make it quick." Molly took a few seconds to gather her thoughts. "Last night I stayed at the resort, as I told you. The first thing I noticed was that Robina McDonald was limping."

"Limping, as in injured?"

"Yes. She hurt her knee, supposedly while walking. Anyway, she also put quite a lot of effort into casting aspersions on Blane Tully. She came to my room to tell me about overhearing an argument between Blane and Devon."

"Molly," he protested, "I can't—"

"I know, it's hearsay. At first I thought she was trying to misdirect me. But Blane keeps popping up. He had an argument with Dr. Dunbar that I overheard while snowshoeing. He wanted to quit doing something and she refused to let him."

"You don't happen to know what he was talking about, do you?" The chief's voice held a hint of humor.

"Unfortunately I don't, but he was angry enough to run away. And it's very possible he was the person who grabbed me. Blane makes chocolates for a living."

"You said the glove over your mouth smelled like chocolate," Chief Thomson said.

"That's right. Do you know where he was during the iceboat race?" The chief didn't reply.

Molly sensed she'd overstepped. "Sorry." She was almost to the college so she said, "I'm also wondering if Dr. Dunbar had something to do with Devon's death. She's been doing nutritional analysis on Blane's chocolates. He uses apricots all the time. She has access to apricot kernels and the knowledge of how to use them."

"Molly, we checked the food kitchens and came up empty."

"Blane's kitchen, then? Or the college chemistry labs?" Molly saw the Superior Bay College entrance and slowed, signaling. "Anyway, it's all food for thought. I'm at Superior Bay right now to check on Bridget. She's been out of touch and I'm worried."

"I'll let you go, then. You've given me a lot to think about, Molly. I appreciate your hard work."

"Thanks, Chief Thomson. I'm hoping this gets wrapped up soon."

"From your lips to God's ears. Call us if you need us, Molly."

Molly said goodbye and disconnected. She tried to remember if she knew where the chemistry lab was as she crawled along the drive. Like most campuses, this one was a maze of buildings. She should park and check a directory on her phone.

She found a visitor spot and sat, engine running, to pull up the college website. The science building was a short distance from this lot, so she switched off the motor. Bundled up students crisscrossed the campus, wearing backpacks and carrying phones. At the science building, a young man held the door open for her.

"Where are the chemistry labs?" she asked, figuring that would be easier than wandering the halls.

"Second floor," he said. "Rooms 210 through 214."

"Thanks," Molly said, slipping past him into the warm building. She found the stairwell and climbed up to the next floor. Lines of doors extended down the corridor, numbers posted on the wall.

Each door had a gridded window, so she was able to peer into the labs as she searched for Bridget. She found her in Room 212, standing by herself near a workbench, goggles on. The room held several benches, a whiteboard, cabinets, safety sinks, and a selection of lab equipment. Molly had an immediate flashback to her high school days.

She opened the door and stepped in. "Hi, Bridget."

Bridget gave her a huge smile. "What are you doing here?" She frowned down at something in her hand. "You must have been reading my mind." On the counter nearby, a Bunsen burner gently hissed, heating something in a tall beaker.

"Really? What's that?" Molly went around the bench to Bridget's side.

Bridget extended her gloved palm, which held a fragment of pale tan shell. "It's an apricot pit. Or part of one."

Molly's pulse leaped. Her theory about someone using a chemistry lab to make poison had been confirmed. "Where did you find that, Bridget?"

"On the floor." Bridget pointed to the floor near her feet. "They missed it when they cleaned the room. All I know is that we don't use apricots in our experiments."

Had someone been working on another batch of poison? "How do you make cyanide from apricot pits anyway?"

"You take off the shell and process the kernel inside." Bridget set down the pit and walked toward a cabinet. "The water reflux method uses citric acid." She opened the door. "There's an open container of it in here."

The door handle rattled and Dr. Dunbar stepped in, carrying a tote. "What are you doing in here? I reserved this room."

Bridget's spine stiffened, but she merely said, "I'm working on an experiment for class. This is the lab I usually use." She casually closed the cabinet door, nudging Molly away. Meanwhile, Molly's heart was pounding. Would Dr. Dunbar guess what they were really up to?

At first, it seemed not. Dr. Dunbar stepped farther into the room, setting her bag on a workbench. "You really should check the reservation schedule online, Bridget."

Bridget sent Molly a helpless shrug. Molly guessed that either she hadn't checked the schedule or Dr. Dunbar hadn't entered a reservation.

"Can't you both work in here at the same time?" Molly asked. "What difference does it make?"

"I prefer privacy," Dr. Dunbar said. "A lot of people depend on accurate results from the work I do." She glanced over at Bridget's station and froze.

Dr. Dunbar had noticed the apricot shell.

Her movements were jerky as she approached Bridget's area. Then she glared at Molly and Bridget, ugly rage moving over her features. Seeing they had noticed, she struggled to get her expression under control. "What's that?" she asked with a clearly forced laugh.

Bridget picked it up with two fingers. "This? It's proof that you killed Devon. Who's next on your list, I wonder?"

Molly sucked in a breath, awed by Bridget's audacity. Trying not to be obvious, she felt for the phone in her pocket.

The professor's rage returned and Dr. Dunbar wildly scanned the lab with her fists clenched. Then in a sudden rush, she grabbed a jar and threw its liquid contents onto the Bunsen burner. Molly expected the liquid to extinguish the fire, but flames shot up toward the ceiling, quickly spreading along the tiles.

The lab was on fire.

19

The lab door slammed behind Dr. Dunbar and the flames shot along the ceiling and down the workbench toward the floor, anywhere droplets of the volatile liquid had landed. One thing was clear. The route to the door was blocked.

"Molly, I'm so sorry!" Bridget wailed, panic lacing her voice.

"It's not your fault, Bridget," Molly said. "She's a homicidal maniac." She spotted Bridget's phone peeking out of her pocket. "Call 911."

Molly raced over to where a fire extinguisher hung on the wall and pulled it from the clip. She glanced at the directions, the words barely penetrating. Meanwhile, a fire alarm was going off. Maybe a 911 call wasn't needed, but it couldn't hurt.

Bridget was speaking into the phone, frantically telling the dispatcher the situation. Molly pulled the pin from the extinguisher and fired it, but the stream was thin and weak. *Seriously?* She shook it and tried again, with no more luck than she'd had the first time. And shouldn't there be sprinklers? Why weren't they coming on? Perhaps spraying water on a chemistry lab fire was a bad idea.

The fire had leaped to an adjacent counter, where it was eating up the wood. The temperature in the room was rising, becoming almost unbearable. Chemical-laden smoke was curling through the air, as great a danger as the flames.

"We need to get out of here!" Bridget cried.

"How?" Molly asked. She tossed aside the fire extinguisher. The main entrance and a door to an adjacent classroom were both blocked.

"Out the window." Bridget reached for the latch. "But we need to do it fast. Fresh oxygen will make the fire burn hotter and faster."

"But we're on the second floor." Molly pressed close to the window, peering through the glass. If they jumped out, even into a snowbank, they could break their legs or worse.

"We can get to that tree," Bridget said, pointing to a huge maple similar to the one that had hidden Marla's remains for over a decade. The tree was close to the building, and one thick branch extended toward them, almost touching the wall.

"I can't do that," Molly said, her knees quaking.

"You can," Bridget said. "I'll go first and help you. We can scoot along the branch to the trunk. And by then, the fire department should be here."

A billow of oily, evil-smelling smoke engulfed them, and they coughed.

"I guess you're right," Molly said, her voice rasping. "Lead on."

Bridget unlatched the window. She slipped out, reaching for the branch. She was able to clamber out onto it and pull herself along.

Sirens were wailing down on the main road and Molly could see flashing lights. Help was on the way.

With amazing agility, Bridget rotated on the branch to face Molly. She gestured urgently.

Here we go. Not thinking about the drop to the ground, she focused on Bridget's face instead.

"Come on," Bridget called. "You can do it."

Molly practically launched herself at the branch, scrambling and clutching its rough bark. By some miracle, she found herself astride the limb, facing Bridget.

"I did it." Molly felt woozy from the smoke, the panic, and the fact that she was in a tree fifteen feet off the ground. "Now what?"

Bridget was already inching toward the trunk. "There's another branch underneath we can step onto. Or you can wait. The fire department is almost here."

A Loch Mallaig Volunteer Fire Company truck pulled into the parking lot, followed by a police cruiser. Students were pouring out of the adjacent buildings to watch the fire.

"You need help up there?" one young man called. "We can get a ladder."

"I think we can make it," Bridget said. "Come on, Molly."

Molly followed her lead, edging along the branch. When Bridget reached the trunk, she swung her leg over and carefully stepped down to a lower branch. From there, she was able to sit and then swing to the ground.

By the time Molly reached the trunk, there was a circle of young men staring up at her. "We'll catch you," one promised.

"I hope it doesn't come to that." Molly paused to catch her breath and steel her courage for the next move. She sat with both legs on the same side and braced herself, then, gripping the branch, felt around for the one below.

In one swift move, she twisted, swung down, and sat on the branch below. After taking a short break to gather herself, she repeated the motion, dropping to the ground.

She landed with a jolt, but thankfully she'd remembered to bend her knees. Her palms stung from the rough bark.

"You did it." Bridget hugged Molly. "Amazing."

"Hopefully the last time I ever have to do that," Molly said. She looked at the young men. "I appreciate your offer to catch me."

The firefighters had already extended a ladder up to the burning classroom and were spraying foam into the room. Other firefighters with packs were running into the building. Although Fergus was a fellow volunteer, he wasn't on call that day, and Molly was glad he wouldn't be in danger.

"I hope she doesn't want us to catch her too," one of the students near Molly remarked. "That's a bit larger of a drop than we're really prepared for."

Everyone stared up at the four-story building. Dr. Dunbar was poised on the rooftop, staring down at them.

Molly grabbed Bridget's arm. "What is she doing?" Instead of leaving the building, she'd climbed up two more stories.

Chief Thomson arrived at a trot. "Who called in the fire?"

Bridget waved. "I did. Molly and I were in the lab when Dr. Dunbar confronted us and then threw ethanol onto my Bunsen burner. I found a piece of apricot shell that proved she used the lab to make cyanide."

"That's her up there, right?" Chief Thomson asked, then moved away a few paces and spoke into his chest radio. Another officer ran up and handed the chief a bullhorn.

"Dr. Dunbar," Chief Thomson called up. "Please come down, for your safety."

"No," the professor shouted, her voice carrying surprisingly well. "It's over. All of it."

"It doesn't need to be," the chief said. "Please. Step away from the edge of the roof. We'll talk, you and I."

"It's too late," she said. "I killed them. I didn't mean to, but I'm sure they're dead."

The crowd gasped and murmured. Chief Thomson spoke to a couple of officers, who ushered the crowd back away from the scene. Molly and Bridget were allowed to stay. Up in the classroom, the flames were dying down and the black smoke was thinning out.

"If you mean Molly and Bridget, they're okay," Chief Thomson said. "They're right here with me."

Molly stepped closer to the chief, waving, as did Bridget.

"I'm sorry." Dr. Dunbar stared down at them. "One thing keeps leading to another. I can't go on this way."

"It happens to the best of us," the chief said. "Please, for your own safety—"

"My safety means nothing," Dr. Dunbar said. "First Marla, but she was an accident. Then Devon. Why did he have to figure it out? He'd still be alive if he hadn't."

"I hope you're getting all this, Chief," Molly said. "She's confessing to the murders."

Chief Thomson set his jaw. "We're recording it." He raised the bullhorn again, but before he could speak, two officers appeared on the roof. They swiftly grabbed Dr. Dunbar and pulled her away from the edge.

"Whew. That's over." The chief pulled out a bandanna and wiped his forehead. "Talk about a tense situation. I wish we'd had time to call a trained negotiator."

"You did great, Chief." Molly sagged in relief, leaning heavily against Bridget. "It's over. It's really over." Not only had Carol been cleared, the real killer was in custody and had made a confession.

A few minutes later, Officers Murdoch and Drummond emerged from the building with a handcuffed Dr. Dunbar between them. The chief went over to intercept them, and Molly and Bridget followed.

"Take her to the station and book her," Chief Thomson said. "I'll be there soon as the scene here is wrapped up."

"Will do, Chief," Officer Murdoch replied.

The two officers started moving again, but Dr. Dunbar resisted, digging her shoes into the snow. Fastening her gaze on Molly, she said, "I suppose you're wondering why I did it."

Molly certainly was wondering, at least regarding Marla. The motive for killing Devon was pretty clear. He'd learned something about Marla's death and she'd killed him to prevent it coming out. To throw the police off, she'd framed Carol.

Without waiting for a response, Dr. Dunbar continued, "It was an accident. We had an argument early that morning. I pushed her and she fell and hit her head. I was in a panic and didn't know what to do. I didn't mean for her to die."

"So you hid her body under the tree," Molly said, hoping the chief was getting this on tape too. "What were you arguing about?"

"She found out I'd been plagiarizing my work, and she threatened to turn me in." Dr. Dunbar screwed up her features as if forcing out her next words. "To be totally honest, she gave me a chance to come clean. But I couldn't afford to get kicked out. I didn't have anyone to help me the way Marla did. Her grandmother left her all kinds of money. Plus she was totally brilliant and barely had to study. How is that fair?"

"You switched papers with Marla in Dr. Pryde's class," Molly surmised aloud, and Dr. Dunbar nodded. "How did Devon figure out you killed her?"

Dr. Dunbar huffed. "I wish he'd kept his mouth shut. He'd seen me near the maintenance shed that morning, right after I returned the shovel. But at the time everyone thought Marla had drowned, so he swallowed my lie that I was out for an early morning stroll to clear my head. But when Marla was found, he decided to ask me again." She shook her head. "Big mistake."

Molly still had questions. "But what about Blane? Where does he fit in?"

"Oh, Blane." Dr. Dunbar rolled her eyes. "What a loser. He hired me to analyze his chocolates and I found out that he's using all kinds of nasty additives. How dumb is that? He's been paying me to keep that quiet, so when I needed a little help, he was most agreeable." She smirked briefly. "But you, Molly Ferris, are unbelievably persistent.

Anyone else would have run screaming for the hills. But no, you kept digging and digging. I guess my story about Marla being afraid of someone encouraged you rather than just take the heat off me. And obviously you've taught Miss Ross here the same annoying habits." She shook her head in disgust.

"She has indeed," Bridget said with pride. "That's how I found the apricot pit that proves you used the college lab for your nefarious deeds."

Dr. Dunbar glanced up at the lab window, now blackened with soot. "Too bad it's gone. What a shame."

Grinning, Bridget reached into her pocket and pulled out the piece of shell. "Don't worry—it's right here. Not the best chain of custody, nor as condemning as your confession, but it backs up my statement."

Molly studied her employee with amazement. "We were trapped in a burning lab and you thought to save that? I'm impressed."

Bridget beamed with pride. "I learned from the best. You."

Molly laughed. "Most of the time I fly by the seat of my pants."

Chief Thomson cleared his throat. "To clarify a couple of points, Dr. Dunbar," he said, "are you asserting that Blane Tully is responsible for assaulting Molly outside the changing room, and for tailgating her?"

She nodded.

"How about hitting Cole Keith and stealing his iceboat?"

"No, that was me," the professor replied smugly, and Molly fleetingly thought Robina must have been telling the truth about hurting her knee when she fell on the ice. "I'm quite good at sailing, aren't I? I wasn't actually going to hit them. I merely wanted to scare them."

"You're not as good as you'd like to think," Molly said sternly. "If Fergus hadn't been such an expert at it, you would have hit us whether you meant to or not."

"Regardless, you assaulted a man and stole an iceboat," Chief Thomson said. "We'll be adding those charges." He spoke into his chest radio, asking an officer to pick up Blane Tully and bring him to the station.

Molly was glad that Blane would also answer for his misdeeds, but there was one more thing she wanted to know. "Why did you frame my friend? Carol MacCallan never did anything to you."

Dr. Dunbar shrugged. "She used apricot filling, which was what I needed. Plus her chocolates had a very distinct design, which meant they wouldn't be traced back to me. I didn't even know they were hers until afterward."

Molly supposed she understood the woman's logic, but it still rankled. Still, the most important thing was that Carol was no longer a murder suspect. "You get that, Chief?"

"I already called the prosecutor's office, Molly," the chief said. "Carol is officially cleared. Ready, officers?"

As the police officers and the chief escorted Dr. Dunbar toward a cruiser, two vehicles pulled into the parking lot, tires squealing. Fergus had arrived in his Range Rover, and Carol and Laura were in Carol's Chrysler. Doors burst open, and all three ran toward Molly and Bridget.

Fergus swept Molly into a big hug. "I was at the bakehouse when we heard about the fire in the chemistry lab. Since I wasn't on call for fire duty, I didn't get the initial alert. We had to rush over here."

"I'm glad you did," Molly said. "But you missed all the excitement." Now that the danger was over, she could almost laugh about it. "Bridget and I climbed out of that window and down that tree."

"Wow," Carol said. "That must have been quite a feat."

"It's amazing what you can do when you don't have a choice," Molly said with a shudder.

"How did the fire start?" Laura asked, her face anxious.

Between Molly and Bridget, they told the others about the

confrontation with Dr. Dunbar and how she'd deliberately set the lab on fire and fled.

"It was only Bridget's quick thinking that saved us," Molly said. "I couldn't get the fire extinguisher to work right and the doors were blocked by flames."

Bridget ducked her head, blushing, when the others heaped praise on her. "We were lucky there was a tree right there. Otherwise, we would have had to cling to the ledge until the fire department came."

Molly felt woozy at the idea. "Thank goodness for that tree, then."

The chief returned. "Molly, Bridget, if you want to give your statements tomorrow at the station, that will be fine. Why don't you go home and take it easy? You deserve it after that ordeal."

"We will," Molly said. "See you in the morning." She blew out a huge breath after the chief walked away. "I can't believe it's over. I almost don't know what to do with myself."

"There's an ice dancing contest at the faire tonight," Carol said. "The last event. Want to grab something to eat there and watch? If you feel up to it, I mean."

"Ice dancing?" Bridget said. "I'm in."

"Sure, I'll go," Molly slipped her arm through Fergus's elbow. "Maybe we'll pick up some moves for the Valentine's dance."

"Sounds good," Fergus said, smiling down at her. "My best kilt just came back from the dry cleaner, so I'm ready."

At the sight of his smile, which she'd thought she might never see again, Molly felt woozy once more, but this time it was in a good way. As he escorted her to her vehicle, her spirits soared. Once again, the Bakehouse Three—this time including Bridget—had solved not one, but two murders, and brought a killer to justice.

All was right in Loch Mallaig again.

20

With the time to get ready for the Valentine's dance approaching, Molly set aside the novel she'd been reading. She edged over an inch on the sofa, preparing to extricate herself from beneath Angus's head, which was firmly planted on her leg. Then her cell phone rang, the bright jingle she'd assigned to her daughter, Chloe.

"Hello, sweetie," Molly said, sitting back again. "Did you get the chocolates I sent?"

"Eating one right now," Chloe said. "You made these? They're fantastic." Instead of the Tully's chocolates she'd originally bought, Molly had sent an assortment of her own handmade truffles to her parents and Chloe.

"I did. Laura, Carol, and I took a class." *And then some.*

"I'm impressed, Mom," Chloe said. "So what else is new?"

Molly sat back with a laugh. "Where to begin. Valentine's Day dance or murder case?"

"Mom!" Chloe scolded. "I can't believe how many murder cases you get involved in. I couldn't believe it when I read about Devon Macintosh on the national news. And there you were, right in the middle of it. I assume that's the case you're referring to."

"Yes. And I never plan such things, believe me." Molly launched into a recap. "Since we last talked, Blane Tully has been arrested. I think he'll get a reduced sentence for testifying against Brianne Dunbar. He says now that he had suspected her, and when she insisted that he try to scare me, he was positive."

Chloe snorted. "But he didn't come forward. He just did her bidding."

Molly ran her fingers through Angus's fur. "He was too worried about keeping his business afloat. And after Devon stole his family recipes, he wasn't all that broken up about his death, I gather. Devon's assistant, Robina, and his cameraman, Cole, were also strong suspects. His death stemmed from the discovery of Marla Bannerman's bones, though."

"And you were right there when that happened too, right?" Chloe said. "It's good that poor Marla can finally be put to rest."

"It is," Molly said. "Local residents did a fundraiser for a grave and headstone, and she'll be buried in the cemetery here next spring. She didn't have any family, which is sad, so we stepped in."

"People in Loch Mallaig always rise to the occasion." Chloe was quiet for a moment. "Are you happy you moved there, Mom? Apart from the murders, I mean."

Molly thought about Loch Mallaig, its wonderful people, her great business partnership with her best friends, and most on her mind right now, her relationship with Fergus MacGregor.

"I am more than happy. It's home now," Molly said with a smile. "Would you have time for a visit soon?"

"Soon, I promise. And now I've got to go."

"Have a great day, Chloe. Love you."

"Love you, too, Mom."

Right before her daughter hung up, Molly heard something in the background that gave her pause, like a voice making announcements at a bus station or airport. But she brushed it aside, thinking she'd misheard, and levered her body off the sofa at last.

"And now I'm going to take a bath, Angus." Her heart leaped in excitement at the thought of the evening ahead. "And get ready for my Cinderella transformation."

Molly had built in time for a leisurely hot bath. Afterward she showered, washed her hair, and blow-dried it. Then she put in hot rollers to give her hair some body and curl. Next came a full application of makeup, from foundation to eyeliner to lipstick. Admiring her reflection, she admitted that the result was attractive, but she couldn't imagine doing this every day. No, the natural look was fine with her. A glance at the clock told her it was time to put on her dress.

Fergus was coming to get her, which Molly thought was nice, especially since the dinner was at the resort. But he had insisted, wonderful man that he was.

As she walked to her closet, Molly drifted off into memories of special times with Fergus. She was so glad that they had been close friends for years first. They genuinely liked each other. They laughed a lot, often about the silliest things. She trusted him. Relationships like theirs didn't come along very often. And after one happy marriage, Molly knew how blessed she was to experience love again.

Molly removed the silver-and-white dress from the hanger and slipped it on. It was almost weightless yet so flattering, probably one of the loveliest dresses she'd ever owned.

She donned the new silver shoes, though she would change out of them and into boots after Fergus saw her outfit. She wanted to give him the full effect when he first came to the door—before covering herself with weather-appropriate coat and gloves. No hat tonight, though. She could suffer some chill to prevent mashed curls.

Molly and Angus were waiting at the front window when Fergus arrived. The little dog had been surprisingly good at not stepping on, clawing, or getting dog hair on her new gown. Leaving the engine running, Fergus came upstairs to get Molly.

She opened the door and stepped back so he could take her in. He whistled. "Molly, you are spectacular."

"You like it?" Molly spun around so he could view the entire dress.

"I love it." He swept her into his arms and almost kissed her, then pulled back. "Oops. I don't want to smudge your lipstick."

"I can reapply it if I need to," she said, turning up her face.

He grinned and obliged—carefully. Then he examined her lipstick. "Okay. No smudging."

"I wasn't worried. I've been excited for this evening for weeks," she told him as she slipped her shoes off and put them in a bag.

"Me too." He helped her into her winter coat and held the shoes and her evening bag while she put on boots and gloves. "All set?"

"All set." She said good night to Angus, then preceded Fergus out the door and down the stairs, glad she wasn't navigating them in the silver heels. "What a beautiful night." The air was crisp and clear, but it wasn't quite as frigid as it had been the last few weeks.

"It certainly is," Fergus said as he came down the stairs behind her. He slipped ahead and opened the passenger door for her. Then they were off to the resort.

Whatever had been bothering him over the past few weeks appeared to be resolved, Molly noticed. Although he hadn't said much, there was a big smile on his face, and he whistled a jaunty tune. He must be as excited about the dinner dance as she was.

When Fergus and Molly entered the King's Heid Pub, the first person Molly saw was her daughter standing near the hostess station. She was dressed in a gorgeous sea-green gown, and beside her was a handsome young man.

"Chloe?" Molly stopped short, unable to believe her eyes. "But I . . . you . . ." Now the background sounds Molly had heard made sense.

"Hi, Mom." Chloe came forward and gave Molly a warm hug. "I was leaving the airport when we talked. I wanted to surprise you."

Molly was still trying to wrap her head around it. "You succeeded."

"Good." Chloe smiled at Fergus. "Hi, Fergus. Nice to see you."

"And you, Chloe." Fergus held his hand out to Chloe's date. "I'm Fergus MacGregor. Welcome to Castleglen."

"Nice to meet you, sir. I'm Garrett Wilson, a friend of Chloe's." After shaking hands with Fergus, Garrett gave Molly a polite bow.

"Garrett works with me at the clinic," Chloe said. "And when I suggested a quick trip to Loch Mallaig, he was surprisingly agreeable."

"The Upper Peninsula is a wonderful area," Garrett said. "Great fishing and golf. Well, maybe not this time of year, but we can cross-country ski or go for a snowmobile ride tomorrow."

Fergus clapped him on the back. "A man after my own heart. Shall we?" He ushered the ladies ahead of him into King's Heid.

The rustic yet elegant restaurant had been decorated for the holiday in red and white trimmings. Topiaries in pots were decorated with heart ornaments. Strings of lights and garland crisscrossed the room. The tables had been set with red cloths over the usual white linen. Candles glowed everywhere, and a huge fire roared in the massive fireplace.

Molly's party was seated together at a table for ten. Carol and Harvey, Laura and Trent, and Bridget and Neil were already seated there. All the women were glowingly beautiful, just as eager as Molly was for a fun night out in formal wear. The men beamed at their dates, happy to be giving them such an evening.

Everyone got up when they arrived, exchanging enthusiastic greetings and careful hugs to avoid smudging makeup. Molly noticed that Laura and Carol didn't seem surprised to see Chloe. Had they planned this behind her back? If so, it was a welcome treat. She didn't see her daughter nearly often enough.

Other guests were filtering into the dining room, and people circulated, saying hello and stopping to chat.

Chief Thomson, handsome in his kilt, held hands with his wife, Irene, looking resplendent in a green satin gown. Molly made small talk with the chief, a pleasant change from their usual discussions. Greer swung by, gorgeous in navy blue. Her clearly smitten date, part-time Loch Mallaig resident and full-time movie star Rocky Sinclair, must have flown in special for the occasion.

Chloe and Bridget had hit it off, Molly noticed, and she overheard Bridget telling Chloe about her plans to become a forensic scientist. "Hanging out with your mom and the other ladies while they solved a case really cemented it for me," she said with all sincerity. "It's almost like having an internship."

"My mom is pretty amazing," Chloe said. "Sometimes I think she missed her calling." Chloe caught her mother's eye and winked.

After a social hour with appetizers, Fergus made his way to the front of the room, where he joined Grizela Duff, magnificent in burgundy velvet. Alastair Thomson played a short refrain on his bagpipes and the guests moved to their seats.

"Good evening, ladies and gentlemen," Fergus said. "Welcome to Castleglen. We're thrilled to be hosting the Loch Mallaig Valentine's Day dinner and dance this year. As you know, proceeds will go to support our local historical society, which is led by Grizela Duff. I'll let her give us a quick update on the faire. We broke all visitor records this year, I understand. The event was a smashing success."

Grizela gave a mercifully brief update, then Alastair closed the segment with another tune as servers came around with salad. The menu for the evening included a choice of prime rib, salmon, or vegetable lasagna.

Molly was halfway through her salad when a server arrived at her side. "For you, madam." He bowed low, holding a small silver tray with a folded note sitting on it.

"What's this?" Molly asked. "Did anyone else get a note?"

"I didn't," Carol said, her face wreathed in smiles.

"Me neither," Laura said.

Molly plucked the note off the tray and opened it. *Meet me in the gold sitting room. Fergus.* She realized that he hadn't returned to the table. "I'll be right back, ladies," she said, rising to her feet.

She made her way through the dining room and out into the hall, where she soon found the room in question.

"Fergus?" she said as she entered. "What's going on?" Her heart began to pound. Did he have bad news to share, something that couldn't be said in public?

The small space, usually used as a breakout room during conferences, was lit tonight with candles that cast a romantic glow on several vases of roses arranged throughout the room. In the center was Fergus, resting on one knee with a blue velvet box in his hands. As she approached, he flipped it open.

Molly gasped. Inside was a dazzling ring, an antique pear-shaped diamond surrounded by smaller stones set in gold.

Stunned, she stared at Fergus, who was watching her closely, tender emotion shining in his eyes. "Fergus, what . . . ?"

"Molly, since you returned to Loch Mallaig, every day with you has been better than the last. You've brought so much joy to my life, and I want that joy to continue to grow for as long as we live." His voice cracked with emotion, and a hopeful smile spread across his face. "Molly Ferris, will you do me the honor of becoming my wife?"

Molly flushed with excitement, happiness, and love as she took in his words. Fergus wanted to *marry* her. He wanted her to become his wife, his partner in all things. Now she knew why Chloe was here tonight. How incredibly thoughtful of Fergus to invite Molly's daughter, to include her in this momentous event.

She gazed into his handsome face, which she had loved for so long. There was only one answer to his question.

She beamed at him. "Yes, Fergus. I will marry you."

Fergus plucked the ring from the box. "I hope you like this. I got other opinions when I picked it out. Laura, Carol, and Chloe have been helping me with all of this for weeks."

"It's perfect," she whispered. "I love it." Something clicked in her mind. "Is this why you've been acting so strange lately? I've been worried."

He blinked at her in surprise. "Oh, have I? I'm sorry. This has been pretty all-consuming, yes. Allow me to make it up to you." With fingers that trembled slightly, he slid the engagement ring onto her left hand. Then he stood and drew her into an embrace. "I love you, Molly."

"I love you too," she said. "So much."

After a long and fervent kiss, Fergus said, "Shall we return to dinner?" He held out his arm and Molly slipped hers through his elbow.

On the way back to the dining room, Molly felt as if she were walking on air. She and Fergus were *engaged*. Every time her gaze caught on the gorgeous ring, she wanted to shout for joy.

Fergus paused in the doorway. "Do you mind if I tell them?" he whispered to Molly.

"I am certain they already know," Molly replied with a grin. "But go ahead and make it official."

Fergus nodded to Grizela, who tapped her glass with a knife. The room gradually fell silent.

"Ladies and gentlemen," Fergus said. "I have a very important announcement." His expression was so grave that everyone straightened in their seats, riveted. Then he broke into a huge grin. "Molly Ferris has agreed to become my wife."

The room erupted in cheers. Alastair picked up his bagpipes and launched into a lively melody. Dallis Witherspoon and his date got up and began to dance, twining between the tables. More couples from The Leaping Lowlanders followed, twirling and spinning around the room, kilts flying and curls bobbing.

"Did you arrange this?" Molly asked, surprised anew at Fergus's planning.

"I might have called in a favor or two," he answered, squeezing her tightly to his side.

When the celebratory song ended, the dancers all sat down in unison, panting, flushed, and delighted. Alastair put aside his bagpipes and dove into his salad again. Molly and Fergus joined their friends at their table.

Fergus picked up his glass. "To you, my lovely future bride."

Molly raised hers as well. "And to you, my fine husband-to-be."

As they clinked glasses and drank, Molly thought her heart might burst. She was beyond blessed. She had Angus, family, friends, and now Fergus. Her life was complete.